To a dazzling new vampire series for fans of Bella Forrest's

SHADE OF VAMPIRE.

Introducing:

THE VAMPIRE GIFT

by E.M. Knight

www.EMKnight.com

www.facebook.com/AuthorEMKnight

EM@EMKnight.com

Books by E.M. Knight

THE VAMPIRE GIFT:

Currently Available:

The Vampire Gift 1: Wards of Night

Coming Soon:

The Vampire Gift 2: Kingdom of Ash (June 2016)

For an updated list of books, and to see the latest dates for my upcoming releases, check out my website:

www.EMKnight.com

The Vampire Gift 1: Wards of Night

By E. M. Knight

Cover art by B. Wagner

First Edition: April 2016

Book Description

THE VAMPIRE GIFT 1: WARDS OF NIGHT

When 17-year old Eleira wakes up in a strange, unfamiliar room high above the redwoods of California, she has no idea what's waiting for her in the dark.

A trio of hauntingly beautiful vampires with a taste for her blood...

An ancient sanctuary locked away in time...

And a wicked queen determined to do anything to hold on to her rule.

Caught between three vampire brothers and coveted for her bloodline, Eleira is swept into a world of supernatural magic where nothing is as it seems and betrayal lurks behind every corner. She must fight for her survival or risk being made prey for the very creatures who keep her there. But when she discovers a dark, twisted prophecy with her at its center, she is pulled deep into the heart of THE HAVEN... and realizes that the vampires she seeks to escape might just be key to her salvation.

Chapter One

ELEIRA

I wake up with a jolt. Alarm rips through my body. *Where am I?* This isn't my Stanford dorm…

I try to push myself up. My muscles are slow to respond. Everything feels like it's part of a dream. My mind is awake, but my entire body is fuzzy.

I definitely know I'm not at home.

I crane my head up. There's a sharp pain in the side of my neck. I bring my hand to it and wince when I feel a nasty bump.

My fingers run along my skin. The bump is about half the size of a golf ball.

A shiver of fear takes me. *What on earth is going on?*

The cloudiness in my mind starts to part. I'm on a cold, metal floor in the middle of a circular room.

I groan as I push myself upright. I manage to sit up, but my body still doesn't feel like my own.

What's been done to me?

I take a slow look around. It takes me a second to understand that all the surrounding walls are glass. They arc up into a dome, with its center right above my head.

An atrium? A greenhouse? I have no idea...

I put both hands on my neck and roll my head from side to side. The bump is only on one side. It's sensitive. The muscles running up to my jaw are stiff. I open and close my mouth a few times, trying to work out the tension.

That helps a little. There's a pervading chill in the air that's made worse by the metal floor that steals my warmth. I'd try to stand, but I'm not sure my legs would support me.

"Hello?" I call. My voice sounds pathetically weak to my ears. I clear my throat and try again.

"Hello!"

The sound echoes around the room before fading away. The silence that follows mocks me.

I grumble as I look at my body. I'm wearing the same clothes I wore to class yesterday. But there's a stickiness to my skin, a feeling of filth, and it makes me think that more than a single day has passed.

I screw my eyes shut and try to remember. I'd just managed to get through an exhausting week of class. Midterms were coming up, and like the rest of my friends, I retreated to a private room in the library to study. And then —

A flash of red pulses through my mind. I gasp. My eyes pop open.

Just like that, the memory is gone.

I have no idea what happened after I opened my books.

Come on, Eleira, I scold myself. *Think! It's not like you to be helpless!*

But try as I will, nothing comes to mind.

"Hello?" I try again. "Is anybody there? Where *am* I?"

Once more, the only answer is silence.

With a grunted effort I haul myself to my feet. The moment I do, a wave of light-headedness hits. I sway and my vision goes white.

The fit passes. But I'm not left unaffected. That's never happened to me before.

Again my hand goes for my neck. I trace the strange bump and wonder what it is.

I catch my reflection in the far glass wall. I hesitate, then inch toward it slowly, trying to ensure the next step won't send me lurching to the floor.

When I'm less than a foot away, I feel an odd tug on my ankle. I look down and suck in a sharp breath.

There's a silver string stretching to me from the center of the room. It's attached to an anklet fit snugly around my leg.

I bend down and try to rip it off. It's no good. The string is extremely thin, almost invisible, but it's as strong as fishing line. There's no clasp that I can see, and no way I can get it off.

Bizarre.

The window forgotten for now, I walk back to where I woke up. There's a tiny compartment in the floor that I'd overlooked. As I come closer, it reels the string in. When I walk away, it lets it back out — but no farther than the wall.

A surge of panic threatens to take over as the implications sink in: *I'm a prisoner!*

My breathing starts to quicken. I feel the panic rising. My

heart beats faster and faster...

I close my eyes and force myself to adopt a sense of calm. There's no point jumping to conclusions. Especially this soon. For all I know this could be some elaborate prank orchestrated by one of the sororities I wanted to pledge...

But that doesn't feel quite right. Still, it's the only assurance I can give myself at this point.

I open my eyes, and once my body is no longer shaking, I return to the glass wall.

It's pitch black outside. That's the only reason I can see my reflection. The light in the room comes from lamps embedded in the floor.

Keeping my tied foot back, I step forward and lean into the window. I cup my hands in front of my eyes. I think I can make out the barest hint of stars up in the sky. But it might just be my imagination, or my mind grappling for a hint of normalcy about this place. Otherwise, the night is unnaturally dark.

The sound of metal sliding against metal makes me jerk around.

There, on the other side of the room, two of the window

panes have come open. A tall man with jet black hair and sharp, predatory eyes stands in the entrance.

"Hello, my darling," he says in a slow drawl. "Did you miss me?"

And then, without warning, he launches himself at me.

Chapter Two

RAUL

"Hey. Hey, look, she's up!"

My younger brother Phillip points to the screen. My head turns that way, and, sure enough, he's right.

"What a beauty." James drawls behind me.

I grimace without being able to stop myself. Ever since my older brother was introduced to the Vampire Lestat books in the 80's he'd taken it upon himself to embody the fictional prince. He'd even moved down to Louisiana to adopt the accent— something he hasn't dropped since.

I face him, diverting my attention from the young girl on the screen. "Remember what she's here for," I remind him. I eye him up and down. "She's *not* to be your plaything."

James chuckles. "Don't you worry your pretty red head, Raul," he tells me. "I'm not going to do anything against Mother's orders. But —" he steps toward me. "Might I remind you that it was *I* who found her? And it was *I* who brought her here."

"Actually, it was all —" Phillip tries to butt in.

"Silence!" James growls.

Phillip shrinks back.

"It was me, and I won't put up with your snivelling excuses saying otherwise."

My fists tighten. My two brothers have never been on the best of terms. Phillip's subdued, intellectual personality clashes mightily with James's boisterous 'rah-rah-look-at-me' persona.

As for me? I like to think I take on the best of both of them. But that might just be vanity speaking.

"What's that she's doing?" Phillip asks.

I look at the screen. "Looks like she found the chain."

Phillip glances from me to James. "Do you think she's going to break it?" He sounds nervous.

"No," James says confidently. "Not yet. She's not aware of the new powers imbued in her blood."

That seems to alleviate Phillip's concern.

"Besides," James continues. "Even if she does, where would

she go?"

"She looks scared," Phillip says.

Even I bark a laugh at his humanity. "Of course she's scared. Wouldn't you be? Or have you forgotten what it's like to be human?"

"Never," Phillip shakes his head roughly. "I'll never forget what it's like to be them. They are who we *were*, and if we lose that part of us —"

"Ah, Phillip, ever the dreamer," James interrupts. He strolls over and tousles his hair. Then he smacks the side of his head. "If Mother heard your admission, have no doubt, she *would* send you to the dungeons."

James says it so coolly, so confidently, that the threat is easy to miss. But I know my brother well enough to pick up on it.

So does Phillip. He gulps.

I put a hand on both their shoulders. James looks at me with revulsion, whereas Phillip seems calmed by my presence.

"Remember," I remind them both. "Nothing we say or do *ever* leaves this room." My hand tightens so that my point comes across. "Understood?"

Phillip nods, but James only scowls and ducks out of my grip. "Gah!" He spits and speeds out the room.

"Where's he going?" Phillip asks.

"Forgive him," I say. "He needs time to cool off. Anyways, it's not important—"

I cut off when Phillip mutters a curse. My younger brother *never* uses foul language.

"What is it?" I demand.

He points to the screen. James is in the room with Eleira.

I swear and run after my older brother.

Chapter Three

ELEIRA

I scream as the black-cloaked man closes the space between us. He moves so fast I don't have time for any other reaction.

One hand grips me by the neck under my chin. The other curls around my back, forcing my body to his.

"So young," he mutters under his breath. "So very... nubile."

Who are you? What do you want? I try to ask, but the words get caught in my throat. He's cutting off my circulation. All I manage is a feeble croak.

"What's that?" He leans an ear in. "I didn't quite catch that."

Then he laughs, as if it's the greatest joke in the world.

I struggle against him but he's so *strong.* It doesn't help that my body is weak from a pervading sense of deprivation.

His nostrils flame as he brings his face close to mine and takes a deep breath. His eyes roll up in momentary ecstasy.

What kind of monster is this?

Just when I'm certain he's about to force himself on me, pressing his lips to mine, or — I swallow — even worse, a strong voice of command sounds from the entrance.

"Put. Her. *Down*."

My captor freezes. He doesn't release me, but he backs off enough so I can suck in a ragged breath.

"James." The voice continues. "I am telling you to back off."

James, I think. *That's his name. His name is James.*

"And why should I, *little* brother?" The man holding me snarls. "Can't you smell her? Can't you tell how *sweet* she is?"

He spins us both around and thrusts me forward. I gasp in alarm. "Here, Raul," he says. "Have her. I know how much you crave her blood."

Crave my blood? My head starts to spin. What kind of madness is this?

The man in the doorway steps forward. He looks nothing like his brother—if indeed that is what they are. His hair is the deepest shade of red I've ever seen, like the embers of a fire in the night. His eyes — I shouldn't be saying this about my captor, but his eyes take my breath away. They are the most brilliant green possible and framed by long, dark lashes. They lend a fierce intensity to him that cascades down and encompasses his whole body.

Or maybe it's just the way he's looking at me. *At us?*

"Go on," James taunts. His hand wraps in my hair as he pushes me to the door. "Take her! I know you're dying to."

My thoughts blacken and start coming up with all sorts of horrifying scenarios. Rape. Torture. They spoke of blood!

All without me being able to do a damn thing.

"No," Raul says. He doesn't look at me, instead directing his entire gaze at his brother. "She is *not*. To be. Harmed!"

James steps into me. His free hand curls around my waist and splays across my tummy. Revulsion fills me from his touch.

"Who says we're harming her, dear brother?" He sweeps my hair away to expose the side of my neck with the foreign bump. "Just one sip. What's the worst it could do?"

Raul's features twist as he struggles with the suggestion. I can see the temptation clear in his eyes.

"No," I whisper. "Please."

Abruptly he flies at me. James laughs and steps away, leaving me dangling. The speed with which they move is so fast. I start to fall, but then Raul's hands are on me, and he's holding me, tight to him...

I screw my eyes shut and pray that the next moment I'll wake and be free of this nightmare.

No such luck. My heart is pounding so hard I'm afraid it'll rip out my chest.

One second passes. Then two. Then three. Raul's body is cold and hard as stone.

But nothing more happens. I dare to ease my eyes open...

Raul is staring down at me. Through some trick of the light his green irises seem to swirl like smoke caught on an upwind. I blink, and the moment is ruined. The illusion is gone.

But I cannot look away. Something about him captivates me. There's a faint, black circle that surrounds his irises. At that moment, despite all my better judgment, I know that if he asks anything of me, I'll say yes. Whatever he wants, I'll do, if for no other reason than —

"I'll leave you two to get acquainted," James interrupts from the doorway. He steps out and hits a button. The panels slide shut.

The moment he's gone, Raul gasps and breaks away from me. I'm left reeling. He pushes off, hard enough that I stagger back. My knees buckle, and I fall right on my butt.

"Ow," I say. "What —"

But I see that Raul is in no shape to answer. His eyes have gone wild. He looks around the room like a caged animal.

I start to get up but he points a finger at me. He's doing everything he can to not look my way.

"Don't," he warns. "Don't move. You don't know —" he grunts. "You don't know... how hard... this is for me!"

I can almost laugh at the absurdity of the admission. Hard for *him?* What about me? I haven't the slightest clue of what's going on!

Except, of course, that I've landed somewhere far, far outside my element.

Suddenly he turns around. With exaggerated effort he walks to the door. Every single step looks like it's made with a hundred pound backpack strapped to his back.

I reach for the bracelet on my ankle and tug on it, then start to pick myself up —

"No!" Raul almost screams. He flings an arm over his shoulder and again points at me. "Don't move!"

I freeze. He can't see me. How did he know? Step by agonizing step he walks to the door. I watch him, unsure whether to be more wary around him or James. Raul saved me — I think — but that doesn't mean anything if he breaks down now.

He reaches the spot where the panels slide open. His fingers search the smooth glass. "Dammit, James," he mutters under his breath. "Dammit! Damn you and your tricks!"

I cry out in alarm when he raises a fist and slams it against the glass. There's so much force behind the blow that the whole outer structure shakes.

What kind of man is he?

But the glass doesn't break or shatter or crack. Raul hits it again. The dome trembles. Still, the door doesn't open. Still, he's trapped inside with me.

"Come on, Phillip," he mutters. "Come on, come on. You know what this torture is like..."

I'm afraid of saying anything lest I draw his ire. But I can't just sit still. I need answers. I have questions. And I —

I don't get to make good on any of it. A crack appears in the panes, and the two halves start to part. As soon as the barest sliver of space is visible, Raul squeezes himself through.

This is my chance, I think. I grit my teeth against my body's weakness and make a dash for the door.

I don't even get a quarter of the way there before the mechanism reverses, and the doors seal shut. Despair wells up inside — and then I remember the bracelet and the link.

I couldn't have gotten out even if the doors had remained open.

Chapter Four

JAMES

I lie back in my bed, a smirk playing across my lips. I let out a long, satisfied breath and cross my arms behind my head.

A few moments later a pretty blonde emerges from under the sheets. She sidles up higher and snuggles close to me. She runs a hand over my bare chest.

I almost pull away, but I have the presence of mind to remain still. I've never liked these little displays of affection after the act.

But April is important to me, in more ways than I can count... yet none of them at all in the way she hopes.

"So," she says. "Did that make you feel better after the confrontation with your brothers? I don't know why Morgan makes you treat them as equals when you're clearly better... smarter... more handsome..."

She starts to kiss my jaw, but I turn away.

"*Queen,*" I say lazily. "You will refer to her as Queen."

April pouts in a way she thinks softens my heart. In truth, I'd be hard pressed to think of an expression more repulsive. It really does make her look like the simpering eighteen-year-old she is.

"But there's nobody else around, my prince," she says. "Surely in private I can call your mother —"

"By her proper title," I cut in. I grab April's wrist and bring it to my face. My eyes focus on the nearly translucent, throbbing vein on the underside.

She sucks in a breath. I can feel the fear in her. And, of course, the anticipation.

"Do you..." her voice quivers. She puts on a good show of acting confident when outside the bedroom, but I know it all for just a mask. "Do you still need a drink? After..." she swallows, and I can almost hear the tears building beyond her eyes. "After all that we did?"

"Mhmm," I say, lazy, teasing. I feel her pulse quicken, and I know she's truly afraid.

I love playing these sort of games with her.

"A drink, a drink, a drink, a drink..." I say.

"If you must do it then do it quick," she burst out. "Please,

James..."

I release her. "No," I say. "I find I'm not thirsty after all."

She heaves out a sigh of relief. "Oh, thank God —"

"I prefer something much closer to the source," I snarl, and force myself onto her, exposing her neck. She cries out, but my lips are already peeled back, and I sink my fangs deep into her carotid arteries, the one that pumps fresh blood right out of her heart.

My hand flies over her mouth and stifles her screams as I draw the blood out of her. *Sweet, sweet girl,* I think. Aside from the screams she doesn't fight back.

When I've had my fill — but still nowhere close to enough, given how much Eleira's scent has awakened my cravings — I let April go. Her hands dart to her neck as she tries to stem the blood flow. But the wound will heal on its own before she has a chance to bandage it. I made sure of that, by injecting the serum as I withdrew.

"Look, darling," I say. I pull her hands away and spread them in front of her face. "You're not even bleeding. Imagine that!"

"Th — thank you," she stutters.

I scoff a cruel laugh. "Now go on, get out of here. The other humans will start wondering where you've been for so long."

She stammers a few more platitudes as she hitches out of bed. She knows how close I came to taking her life.

But she also knows, I assume, that such is the risk of bedding a vampire.

I watch her cute backside as she goes. Just before she closes the door, I add, with a winning wink, "Not a word of this to anyone, my dear."

She bobs her head up and down, meek and drained of blood now, and closes the door.

I take a few more minutes to myself before standing up and stretching wide.

Today, April... and tomorrow, Eleira, I think.

At least... if my two brothers don't get in my way.

Chapter Five

RAUL

I'm furious as I stalk down the walkway. For James to tempt me like that, and then leave me alone in there, with *her* —

I close my eyes and shudder. It took all the self-control I possessed not to feed. Her blood called out to me like a black-veiled siren in the night. It was unlike anything I'd ever sensed before.

No wonder Mother warned us.

But she also made it absolutely clear that Eleira was not to be harmed. If we are going to use her for the succession, she has to be pure, untouched, untarnished.

A growl comes from deep in my throat. James knows her worth and value as well as I. For him to *flaunt* her like that...

Anger bubbles up inside. If it wasn't for Phillip seeing my struggle through the camera and opening the door, I don't know what I'd have done. Six hundred years of waiting would be ruined, and for what? For my older brother to play his sadistic, twisted game?

No... no, I won't let him catch me off guard again. He may have been turned before me, he might have had those extra five years of human life before we were made into these forever-damned creatures, but that does *not* mean he holds authority over me.

The only reason he thinks he does is the respect I've given him over the long, long centuries.

"Raul!" Phillip exclaims when I enter the surveillance room. "I'm sorry, I would have opened the door sooner, but James, he —
"

"Save it." I shake my head. "You don't owe me an explanation for anything. We both know what a brat James really is."

Phillip's eyes go wide. Of the three of us, he has always been the least comfortable with our vampire nature. He'd even gone so far as to renounce drinking all human blood, when he realized he could exist solely on animal blood, about three centuries ago.

But that conversion had stunted his growth. Whereas James and I continued to get stronger with every passing year — as did all of our coven vampires — Phillip remained trapped as he was at the switch. That explains his deference to us.

Vampires are hierarchical creatures. The only thing that catapults one above another is the strength of their supernatural abilities. Not intellect, not social savvy, not age — just pure, raw, strength.

The fact that James and I are neck-and-neck doesn't help distinguish who should lead one bit.

I collapse on the seat beside Phillip. I can sense his unease, being on the same level as me. Those same natural instincts dictate that weaker vampires should always occupy space lower than stronger vampires.

But he is my brother, and I've always made a point of showing him that I won't forget that.

"Anyway," Phillip clears his throat. "What are we going to do about —" His eyes go to the screen. "*Her?*"

I look up and see the human girl slumped over in the middle of the room. Her shoulders are shaking. *Is she crying?*

"Damn, I thought she'd be stronger than that," I mutter.

"She's been through a lot," Phillip says. "Probably traumatized..."

I give a sour chuckle. "And she hasn't even seen the start of it. Wait!" I go rigid. "Zoom in, zoom in, she's not crying!"

Phillip adjusts the camera.

"She's *shivering!*" I exclaim. "Damn, how cold is it in that room? She still has human blood in her, remember?"

Phillip's eyes widen with realization. He plays with the controls on the computer. "It's, uh —" he swallows. "35 degrees."

"That's frigid for a human!" I say. "No wonder she's... damn, just blast the heat!"

My eyes stay glued to the screen as I watch the girl. I wait and wait as the furnace kicks in. And — to my delight — Eleira unfolds like a blossoming flower as the temperature creeps up.

"That," I say finally, "was a glaring oversight."

"Or," Phillips considers, "maybe it wasn't. James was in here and did something behind my back when I wasn't paying attention. He may have done that on purpose."

I shake my head, both in annoyance and disgust. "He wants to break her."

"I know," Phillips agrees.

"He's twisting the orders we got like the worm that he is." I surge up. "If he thinks this is just another game..." I feel my aggression rising. "If he thinks that I'll stand for this..."

Phillip blinks at me. "You'd go against him? For some girl?"

"She's not *some* girl," I correct. "You know just as well as I do how important she will be."

"She *might* be," Phillip interjects. "We're still not sure if she's the one."

I give him a hard look. "Trust me, Phillip," I say softly. "If you had been in that room instead of me, you'd have no doubt. She *is* the one."

Chapter Six

ELEIRA

The sudden heat blasting from the ducts around the room surprises me. Nonetheless, I'm grateful.

I thought they'd meant for me to freeze to death in here.

After James and Raul left, I tried my hardest to take off the bracelet. But whatever strength was left in my arms was not enough. If I had a sharp object, maybe I could slip it underneath and…

But, no. No good wishing for things that don't exist.

The encounter with the two men has left me shaken. Now I know who my captors are, and I've never seen them before.

I'm sure if I had so much as glimpsed James or Raul in the student body at Stanford, I would have remembered them. They are both very distinctive.

Anxious hours pass as I rack my brain for a way out. I don't see it. The circular dome is extraordinarily strong. Even if I had a piece of furniture to throw at it to break the glass, I know it wouldn't work. I saw how hard Raul had hit it, and the effect it had: none.

Besides, with the string linked to the bracelet around my ankle, I can't pass the circumference of the room anyway.

All I have to help guide me are my memories. But they're not worth jack. It's like a block had been put up on events that transpired after I set up in the library. When I try to think of them, all that comes is that flash of red — and a dull pain in the side of my neck.

I crane my head this way and that and hear my spine crack. The strange bump is almost all gone. I wonder what caused it. The way the two men spoke, I can almost believe the most ridiculous thing:

A bite, from a...

Vampire.

I shudder and shake my head. No. No, that's not possible. I'm just letting childhood fantasies get the best of me. Vampires don't exist. The supernatural isn't real. Whoever is doing this to me is just having a grand time feeding into my fears.

And yet... A memory of a long-forgotten summer comes to

me.

I'm seven. Or maybe eight. My best friend Michael and I are exploring the woods. My dad took us up here, to a remote cabin in the Northern reaches of British Columbia, for a week in the summer. Michael's mom is here, too, but not my own. His dad stayed home as well.

There's a lake close to the cabin. Dad's out fishing on a little boat. He sees me and Michael run along the shore. He waves at us.

"Where you going, princess?" He calls out.

"Michael said he found something cool in the woods!" I exclaim. "We're going to go see!"

My dad laughs. "Don't stray far. There's bears and wolves and all sorts of wild animals out there."

"I know, I know," I say.

Michael tugs my shoulder. "Come on," he urges.

I laugh with him and speed away.

Once we're hidden from view, Michael turns on me. "Are there really wild animals?" he asks, a bit meekly.

I giggle. "Look around, dummy. Do you see any?"

He shakes his head. Michael's always been the cautious one, whereas I was more impetuous.

"Dad's just kidding," I assure him. "Animals don't come out around humans. They're scared of us."

Michael blinks. "Really?" he asks.

"Well, duh. Especially during the day. Now come on, what did you want to show me?"

That gets his excitement back. "It's just over this hill," he points.

I nod, and we both race there, not caring how dirty our feet get in the mud from last night's rain.

We top the crest. "There," Michael points.

Far away, past the overgrown bushes and shrubs, is an enormous stump of a tree. The top is blackened and charred, as if it'd been hit by lightning.

"What is it?" I ask.

His eyes twinkle with newfound mischief. "You'll see." He grabs my hand. "Come on!"

We reach the stump. It doesn't look so special, aside from being big. *Really big, like you could fit a family of gnomes inside.*

I giggle at the thought.

"Here," Michael leads me to the other side. "This is what I wanted to show you."

When I see it, I gasp. There are all sorts of strange markings on the wood. They look like ancient symbols.

Below them, there's a tunnel that leads into the earth.

I give a cry of surprise when Michael drops down and starts to crawl through. I thought I was supposed to be the reckless one.

"Where are you going?" I hiss. I know Daddy would be mad if he found out what we were doing.

"Relax," Michael says with a strange sense of authority. "I've been here before. Inside is something really, really *cool, I promise!"*

That's pretty much all the convincing I need. I get on my hands and knees and follow him.

"It's dark," I say as we crawl.

"I know," he answers. "That's why I brought this."

A flashlight comes to life in his hands.

Suddenly Michael disappears. But then his face pops up in front of me, illuminated by the light. "We're here."

He helps me down, out of the tunnel.

We're in... some type of room. An underground cavern. The walls are made of packed dirt and rocks. The floor is tough mud. There's a little table, and an old — a really old — rocking chair in one corner.

I get goosebumps. "What is this place?" I whisper.

"I don't know," Michael says. "But I don't think anyone's been here in years."

He pauses for effect.

"I don't like it," I say. "Why'd you bring me here?" There's something about the room that feels very much off. It gives bad vibes.

"Look!" Michael exclaims. He rushes forward, leaving me in the dark. I stumble after him, not wanting to show him I'm scared, but not wanting to be left alone, either.

He shines the light on a trapdoor in the floor. He motions for me to lift it.

"Michael, I don't think we should..."

"What, are you chicken or something?" He asks.

I narrow my eyes at him. "No," I say. "But —"

"Bwack, bwack, bwack," he interrupts, making the appropriate chicken clucks. "Bwack bwack bwack bwack. Eleira's nothing more than one big chicken!"

"Fine," I say. "I'll help. But after this, we're going back out."

Michael grins. "Deal."

It takes some effort but we manage to lift the trap door. I cough when a mix of dust and mold puffs out.

Michael shines his light down through the opening. There are stairs.

He looks at me. "Ready?" he asks.

Reluctantly, I nod.

He hesitates for a moment, then sticks out his hand. "So you don't get scared and run away," he explains.

I huff, but in truth, I'm grateful. I take his hand.

Together, we make our way down.

The steps are made of stone. They go a long way. At the bottom, they level out to a flat, smooth floor. It's made of the same riv-

er stones, polished and sanded and pressed together.

Michael shines the light around us.

"Whoa," I murmur. "Now this is cool!"

The walls around us are tall and made of grey stone blocks. They make me feel like I'm inside a castle. There's a shelf in the distance. I see books on it. There's also a table with the stub of a burnt out candle. There's a small cot on the floor, long-since rotted.

I walk to the shelf holding Michael's hand. There are cubbies carved in the walls, and they hold all kinds of curious instruments and objects. There are jagged crystals, bits of rose, measuring scales, metal cups and decanters — I gasp — even a rodent skull or two.

"What is this place?" Michael asks reverently.

I don't answer. My eyes are drawn to the spot just beside the bookshelf. There, I see mystical carvings on the walls. Runes, not unlike the ones I saw outside.

Something pulls me toward them. I release Michael's hand and crouch down. I feel... almost a resonance to them. A type of suction, however faint, that makes it impossible to look at anything else.

"I think," I say carefully. I don't know what draws the words

out of me, except that they feel right. "I think... this is the lair of a witch."

Michael scoffs. "A witch? That's crazy. That's—"

I don't hear the rest of what he says. At that moment, a sort of trance falls over me. The runes beckon. I reach out with one hand, fingers trembling, and trace the outlines of the very first symbol.

A jolt runs up my arm. I gasp. Michael says, "What was that?", but my focus is all on the walls before me. My hand passes to the second symbol, an upside-down triangle with three swirling lines through it.

As soon as I touch it, the ground shakes.

Michael grabs my shoulder. "We should get out of here."

"No!" I jerk back. I've never felt such affinity toward anything in my life. My attention shifts to the final symbol. I have to touch it — I must.

Michael tries to yank me away, but I'm consumed by the need to know what the third symbol will do. I snarl and rip away from him. My fingers brush the intricate lines...

A blazing blue light explodes from the wall. I'm thrown back as if hit by a force field. I land hard on my hip and cry out in pain.

Michael's on the ground beside me, but he's quickly picking himself up. The whole room begins to shake. An earthquake! Dust and gravel rain down from the ceiling.

A huge chunk of rock collapses right in front of the wall. It crashes to the floor not two feet in front of my legs.

I scream.

Next thing I know, Michael is grabbing my arm and hauling me up. He drops the flashlight in the commotion. It hits the ground and breaks.

We're trapped in the dark.

The shaking continues. "This way!" Michael yells. We scrambled blindly toward the stairs. I trip and almost fall but Michael catches me again. He pulls me forward. "Here, here!" he cries.

I find the entrance to the stairs and run up, together with him. The tremors throw us from side to side. I hear more crashing behind us. I know the roof is caving in.

Frantic, we reach the top. We're inside the stump, but it's impossible to see. Fear grips me. I hold on to Michael for dear life. The shaking continues.

"Now where?" I scream.

"I don't know!"

Panic threatens to swallow me whole. We're going to die down here. We —

Suddenly the darkness parts, and for a flicker of a second, I see the way out. It's framed by that strange blue glow.

I grab Michael's hand and race toward it. I shove him into the tunnel and quickly follow.

We both emerge and collapse on the ground. A low sucking noise sounds from behind us. I yelp and jump away, then turn just in time to see the entire stump being swallowed by the earth.

And then it's over. Everything is still. A dreary silence falls over the woods.

It takes both of us a long time to catch our breaths. When we do, Michael asks, "Did that really happen?"

I shake my head. "I don't know," I say.

"That flash of light... what was it? Did you *cause it?"*

I just repeat the same three words. "I don't know."

He looks at me. His expression is hollow.

"Now what?"

I take a deep breath. I look into his eyes. "We can't tell any-
body *about this."*

He nods vigorously. "I agree."

I give him my little finger. "Pinkie swear," I say.

We join fingers and seal the bond. After another few minutes,
we get up and wander back to the cabin, shaken and dazed.

Wow. I look around. I haven't thought of that summer in ages. In fact, I'd pushed the memory so far down that I wasn't sure
if it were real or just part of a dream.

And yet... something about it feels very, very real — and
very, very immediate to what's happening now.

Chapter Seven

JAMES

"You called, Mother?"

The Queen looks at me from her glass throne. I hate the pretentiousness of it, raised high on a dais in the middle of the chamber. If I had my way, I'd tear the whole thing down...

Only to build a greater, bigger one, out in the open where all could see.

"I hear you've found the girl," she tells me. Her eyes wander the space above my head. Not once does she look at me. She *hasn't* looked at me, for the better part of two hundred years.

Not like she looks at Raul, I think in a flash of spite.

"Yes," I say. "She's been taken."

"You were the one to discover her?"

My spine straightens, and my shoulders pull back in pride. "Yes."

"A shame it was you, and not your brother," she says casually, glancing at her long, crystal nails.

A growl of displeasure forms in my throat. I try my best not to make it too loud.

"You're troubled, my son," she continues. "Tell me why."

She's baiting me, I know it. "I'm as good as I ever was," I lie. "Better, in fact. The best I've ever been."

She laughs. It's a high, mocking laugh, and it makes goosebumps crawl down my back.

"I can see into your heart, James," she tells me. "I know the things that lurk beneath the surface."

"Nothing but loyalty to you and our coven," I pledge.

"Oh?" She quirks an eyebrow. "Prove it, then."

My breath catches. But I maintain a calm outward appearance. "Anything you ask."

"I'd like you to go to your father," she says. "And, just in time for the succession..." Her pale eyes land on me. "*Destroy* him."

***

I storm into my brother's keep.

"Raul," I rage. "Is this your idea of a joke?"

I'm livid. Absolutely furious. The request our mother made of me... it's unthinkable.

He looks up at me from the drawings spread across his desk. I hate the smugness that creases the corners of his eyes.

"I haven't the slightest clue," he says, a tad too softly, "what you're talking about."

He watches me calmly. He's in his element here, and I know I'm at a disadvantage when I give into the vampiric darkness. But I can't help myself. Not now.

"You told Mother..." My words come out in an angry hiss. "...*To* send me away. Didn't you?"

"I did no such thing."

"Liar!" I accuse. My eyes flash to the papers on his desk. They're ancient parchments, worn and weathered with age. I scoff in disgust. "And what is this? Are you trying to verify the prophecy yourself?"

"You know as well as I do that this is the year." He gestures in the direction of where we're keeping Eleira. "Her birthday lines up, as do the astrological signs."

"*I* could have told you that," I say, exasperated. "*I* found her. You don't trust me?"

Raul looks me up and down. "It's not a matter of trust, brother," he says. "It's a matter of verification."

"You don't trust my judgment, then," I snarl.

"After your display with the girl? No, I'd say I do not."

"Oh, for the love of —" I fling myself into an empty chair and hold a hand to my eyes. "I was just having a bit of fun."

"You don't know," Raul says, "the amount of control it took for me not to touch her."

A malicious grin forms on my face. "Oh, I know all about it, *brother*," I say. "In fact, I'm disappointed in you. I would have sworn you would have taken a taste."

"And ruin what we've been waiting half a millennium for?" he growls.

I don't react in the slightest to his raised voice. When it's darkness against darkness, evil against evil, rage against rage... I *always* have the advantage.

"The only way you would have ruined it," I say sweetly, "is if you had drained her whole." I give a little shrug. "I was merely offering you a sampling, a little morsel. After all..." I lean toward him, gripping the armrests on either side of me. "...why should I be the only one to have tasted her blood? Brothers share, do they not?"

Raul grunts. I laugh.

"Back to the subject of Mother," I say.

Raul shakes his head and returns his attention to the sheets. "So she's sending you away. What of it? You've gone on plenty of missions for her before. We all have."

"No," I say. "This time, it's different."

Raul seems unconcerned. "They're all the same. Go here, retrieve this artifact. Go there, plant a little rumor in the ear of an ally or a foe. Spread a little discord in one of the other covens. You're not going to miss anything while you're away. We both know the speed with which you work."

I smirk. "Is that a little compliment?"

"You finish the tasks fast," Raul says. "But I never claimed you do them thoroughly."

A rush of fury fills me. I struggle to force it down.

"How dare you," I begin.

"I *dare,*" Raul says, "because of how you mocked me with Eleira today."

I give no reply.

"If we're done?" Raul asks. "I have a lot to do tonight. The celestial charts show that —"

"I don't care what they show," I interrupt. "Mother is sending me to The Crypts. Do you understand what that means? She wants me to *kill* our father."

That, finally, gets his attention.

"No," Raul breathes.

This time, the cruel smile on my face comes entirely of its own accord. "Yes, Raul," I say. "Now you understand."

"Father rules the most powerful coven in Eastern Europe," he whispers. "In the last century, they've gone entirely dark. By now, his could be the most powerful in the world."

He shakes his head. "No vampire has gone inside and come back out."

I lean back, finally satisfied with his reaction. "So you agree that it's not a trifling request."

"I assure you, I am in no way behind it," he says. His defensiveness makes me laugh. "I can speak to Mother on your behalf. If that's what you came to ask..."

"No." I rise. I peel off my coat and drape it over my arm. "I think I'm going to do it. There's a reason the task fell to me."

"This is madness," Raul says. "Going against Father's coven would mean open warfare. The covens haven't fought in centuries. Last time it happened, the bloodbath... it was..."

He trails off, unable to finish the thought.

"Don't tell me you're developing feelings of empathy for all those poor humans," I sneer. "It was *their* blood that was shed, not ours."

"Vampires died in the war too."

"Yes, but how many?" I shrug casually. "A dozen? Two?"

"More than that," Raul says. "Hundreds."

"Even if, so what?" My eyes shine with zeal. "Maybe it's time for a purge. Get rid of the weaker ones. Have the strong survive."

"If you're talking Phillip..." he warns.

"Oh no," I say. "Our youngest brother is safe under your guard." I stroll to his desk. "I wouldn't do a thing to harm him."

I turn around, and walk out the room.

"Wait!" Raul calls. I smile, then smooth my features before turning around.

"Yes?" I ask sweetly.

"Maybe... maybe you misunderstood Mother," he says. "Maybe she wanted —something else."

"Her words were perfectly clear to me," I say. I repeat them verbatim. "She told me to go to Father... and *destroy* him."

Chapter Eight

RAUL

I stare after James a long time once he leaves the room. Then I curse and nearly break the table in two.

Mother wants him to go to Father. Mother wants him to *kill* him.

What sort of madness is this?

The last time two covens fought, the results were catastrophic. Not just for us, but for... the humans.

I would never voice my fears to James. That would expose a weakness, I have no qualms about who I am or what I do, not like Phillip, but still, the unnecessary loss of human lives... it gnaws at me.

How many vampires died in the last battle? Maybe a few hundred. But how many humans were killed when our kind was unleashed onto the world?

Tens of thousands.

I shudder with the memory.

I resolve then and there that I must do everything I can to stop the same from happening.

The first thing for me to do is speak to Mother.

I climb the stairs to her private chamber. I raise my fist to knock on the door, but her voice pre-empts the knock.

"Come in, sweetest."

I exhale in annoyance. I never liked the way she could sense us—and the way we are blind to her.

But that's the way the bond works between a vampire and the one who made him. She's also protected because she, unlike any of the other vampires here, is also a witch.

I open the door. Mother's seated by the vanity, admiring herself in the mirror.

I divert my eyes, bow my head, and press a fist to my heart.

"My Queen," I say.

"Oh, hush, hush," she quells me. "It's just you and I. There are no servants present. No need for such formalities."

I straighten. "Thank you, Mo —" I was going to say *Mother*, but change it to her first name. "— Morgan."

She smiles through the mirror at me. One thing I know that *she* detests is when I call her Mother. It reminds her, I think, of the way things were before we were turned.

But that was a long, long time ago.

"Why did you come?" she asks. "Oh!" She mock-gasps. "I know. You're here to petition on your older brother's behalf."

"So it's true," I say. I didn't doubt James, but to hear it confirmed from the Queen's lips...

"Certainly," she says lightly. She spins around and puts her eyes on me.

They're tinged with red. The faintest ring of it on the outline of her irises.

She's been feeding.

"It's madness to send him to The Crypt!" I exclaim.

She smiles and tilts her head to the side. "Always right to the point, aren't you? What, you don't have time for pleasantries."

"You're avoiding the question," I say.

"And you're challenging your Queen." A spark of hatred

blazed in her eyes. "I could have you in chains for that."

I know it's an empty threat but I drop my head anyway. "I'm sorry," I say. "I forget myself."

"Forgiven," she announces with absolutely no conviction. "I've missed seeing your face, Raul. I wonder why you don't visit me more often."

You know perfectly why, you scheming witch, I think.

I keep my expression blank.

She stands and makes her way to me. I'm rooted in place. She reaches up and tousles my hair.

"Flame red," she whispers in my ear. I feel her breath on my skin. "Such a rare quality for a vampire. Almost enough..." she traces her hand along my jaw, "...to tempt even the Queen."

"Enough." I say, and step away.

She was turned, as a human, when she was only twenty. She waited until her children were grown before infecting them with the curse. James was 'older' than her when he was made. I was one year younger. Phillip, with the two years between us, was seventeen.

It's only in the last few decades that her flirtatious games have increased. I always thought them revolting. She treated them as nothing more than a great joke.

Morgan gives me a secretive smile and wink. "Not even the tiniest bit tempted?" she asks.

Disgust floods through me. "No."

"A pity," she says. "We would have *so much fun* together."

"Fun?" I say. "You speak of *fun*, when you go and send your oldest son to start a war?"

"Oh, I very much doubt it'll come to that." She returns to the mirror. "If anything," she adds softly, "It could remind Logan how much he misses me."

I can't help myself. I bark a laugh. "We're nearing five hundred *years*, Mother," I say. "I doubt he remembers you exist."

"Silence!" she screeches. It's a rare outburst. "You will *not* speak of my husband that way!"

"You sent James to kill him," I deadpan. "I seriously doubt he'll view that as a romantic gesture."

"Oh?" she accuses. "And what do you know about love? You, who's never even been with a girl —"

"That's not true," I growl.

"One wench two hundred years ago doesn't count."

Liana.

Before I know what's happening I shoot across the floor and pin Morgan to the wall. I grip her throat, hard. My other hand hovers threateningly over her heart.

"I could kill you, witch," I hiss.

"Oh?" She cranes her chin up, giving me easy access. "Then do it, *son.* Rip my heart out. End your Queen. See what happens when the subjects of our coven turn on you."

I'm breathing hard, lost in the darkness, lost in my rage.

"Do it," she whispers. "End my life. Do it now!"

Suddenly, the gravity of what I'm doing hits me. I release her and stagger back.

"Just as I thought," she sneers. "All talk and no action. Unlike your brother James. I was right in my decision to send him over you."

I look wild-eyed around the room. *What have I done?* But the way she spoke about Liana, the only girl I've ever loved...

"Leave me," she says. "I can tell you are in no state to continue this conversation." She adjusts the bodice of her dress. "Tomorrow you will take the girl out on the grounds. Show her what awaits her if she conforms… and, what will happen if she resists."

Chapter Nine

ELEIRA

Is it ever day here? I wonder.

I don't know how long I've been penned up in this place. I've tried yelling, I've tried screaming, I've tried waving at the camera I'm sure is in the ceiling. I'm scared and lonely and confused. My fingers keep brushing over the spot on my neck. The bump is gone, but now I can feel the tiniest two pinpricks on my skin. Like a spider bite, or a...

A vampire's kiss.

I shake my head to dispel the notion. Once more I'm letting childhood fancies get the best of me.

I wish I had a mirror. Or a clock. Or a phone, or something — anything! — that would get me an understanding of what's happening.

I look at my reflection in the faraway glass. It *feels* as if enough time had passed for the sun to rise. But, it's still pitch black out there.

Could the window be tinted?

I curl up and sleep for an hour or two. My stomach rumbles with hunger. I press a fist into it and do my best to ignore the sensation.

How the hell did I end up here? I think. *Why me?*

At some point during my nap the doors slide open.

My back is to the entrance. My body tenses. I want to look, but I don't want to appear too eager. Whatever these people want from me, I have every intention to resist.

I wait. Silence. The doors close. I hold my breath, hoping to catch sound of whoever had just entered.

But I hear nothing. Carefully I turn my head around — and see *him.*

Raul. He's standing a foot away from the entrance. His whole body is tight. His green eyes lock with mine, and there's such fire there that it makes me gasp.

That breaks the spell. Stiffly he walks over and reaches down to pick me up. I flinch away.

He stops. Then, instead of grabbing me, he holds out his hand.

"I think you've been here long enough," he says. "This room is not meant as your permanent home."

"*Permanent* home?" I stare at him incredulity. "My permanent home is back at the university, in the dorms, with my friends!"

He snorts a chuckle. "Not anymore." He looks at his outreached arm. "Now, are you going to come willingly, or do I have to force you?"

I cross my arms and pull my knees up. "I'm not going anywhere," I announce, "until I understand what's happening. Who are you? Are you from one of the secret societies at Stanford? Is that what this is, some sort of initiation?"

Raul frowns. "*That's* the impression you have?"

"You helped me against the other man. Why?" All the pent-up words are pouring out of me. "And I demand you let me go."

This time Raul's eyebrows go way up. "You *demand?*" he asks. There's a note of stark amusement in his voice. "Really, Eleira, after all you've been through, you think you have any right to make a demand?"

I sniff and hold my chin high. "If you think this a game, I'm not playing. And while you're here I need you to take this off, too."

I jiggle my foot. "I don't like being restricted."

"Yes, well, that we can do," he mutters. I blink, and he's gone from the spot he was standing in. A fraction of a second is all it takes for him to get to the center of the room.

He dislodges the wire. "How did you do that?" I marvel. I know it's not my imagination, or my sleep-deprived brain making things up this time. "How did you get from here —" I point at the ground, "— to there —" I point at him "— so fast?"

"What, like this?" he asks. In a flash he's right back at my side. I yelp in surprise.

"Yes, like that!" I say. My heart is racing. The deep-down suspicions I have about this man are coming to fruition.

"Humans can't move that fast," I whisper.

"My dear Eleira." He kneels down, and his face is finally level with mine. "Whatever gave you the impression that I am human?"

Chapter Ten

Raul walks purposefully ahead of me. I have to step quickly to keep up, because his strides are long and deep.

Since his last declaration, he hasn't said a word. I've tried engaging him in conversation, but it's like talking to a brick wall.

So, I'm left to stew and boil in my own thoughts.

The glass-domed atrium exits to a long, dark hall. The lights are so dim I can barely see Raul's form. But his steps are sure and confident, like those of a man who's walked these corridors many times before.

Well, duh, I think. *This is his home… or laboratory… or facility… or whatever.*

It's chilly everywhere. I start shivering as we advance through hall after hall after hall. There are no windows, and it almost feels like we're inside some massive bunker.

But the layout is way too grand for that.

"Where are you taking me?" I ask in exasperation. "Why am I here? Who *are* you?"

Nothing but silence greets me.

Stubborn man, I think.

Just as we're about to turn a corner I plant my feet. "I'm not taking another step," I declare, "until you tell me what's going on."

Raul stops. He turns back and looks at me.

I suppress a gasp. For a split second, his eyes actually seem to *glow* in the dark.

Of course that's madness. I tell myself. But the memory of my time in the woods comes up unbidden, and I wonder... *Is it?*

"I'm taking you outside," he says stiffly. Something is off about his behavior.

Then I realize what it is; he never actually *looks* at me when he speaks. His eyes go to the space just about my head, or to the side of my body.

Why won't he make eye contact?

"Outside, where you'll let me go?" I ask. "If this isn't an initiation, then I'm sure it's some type of game show." I wave my arms in the air. "Hello! Okay, you got me, *ha ha*. Fun time is over. The camera crews can all come out now." I think of the Stanford Prison Experiment and wonder if this is some type of modern rendition of that.

Raul shakes his head and turns away. "Come."

"No. This isn't funny. And I'm not scared." I try to give credence to the lie by flipping my hair back. "I know you won't do anything to me because—"

My words catch in my throat as Raul spins around and shoots at me. My back strikes the wall. He leers down at me, both hands on my arms, pinning me in place.

Fear rips through me. He's so much stronger than I am, and I'm entirely at his mercy.

What's he going to do?

My breaths are coming quick and shallow. His body presses against mine.

His eyes are locked solely on my neck.

"Don't," he growls. "Ever. Do that. Around me."

Everything about him is straining. His fingers grip tightly onto my arms. I'm going to bruise. I know it. I can't feel his breath, nor his heartbeat, nor any sort of heat from his body.

That terrifies me more than anything else.

Suddenly he lets me go. I fall forward. He glares at me, still not into my eyes, but the hate inside him is palpable.

"Why are you doing this?" I whisper.

"Because you give me reason to," he says. Then, with extraordinary effort, he turns away.

"It'll be better outdoors," he assures me. "There, your scent won't be so tempting."

Chapter Eleven

RAUL

I've scared Eleira. And I hate myself for doing so, but I truly could not control myself.

When she flipped her hair back... and exposed her precious, fragile neck... the neck with James's bite mark still on it — I lost it.

I had to feed. I had to have her. But I could not, for it would destroy the process we've been waiting so long for.

With James's venom already in her system, the infusion of mine would surely kill her.

Now she's more frightened of me than she knows. She tries to hide it, but the emotions of a girl her age are transparent to me.

The sooner I remove myself from her vicinity the better it'll be, for both our sakes.

We walk in silence the rest of the way to the elevator. I hit the button, and it comes up.

We both step inside.

Eleira looks around warily. "Where are you taking me?"

"The ground floor," I tell her as the elevator reaches our destination. The doors come open into the heart of the village. "Welcome to The Haven."

Chapter Twelve

ELEIRA

My eyes go wide when the elevator doors open. The sight before me is like nothing I could have imagined.

We're standing at the base of a tree. It's a giant redwood, with the elevator built right into its trunk.

A cobblestone path opens before me. Thatch roof buildings, none of them more than two stories high, line either side. Some have large, gated estates, while others are more modest.

I see farm animals strolling around. Chickens, sheep, cows… but no people.

All the houses are dark. I look up, expecting to see stars… but find only a dense canopy of branches above me. Although, here and there, the occasional patch of dark sky is visible.

I take one look at Raul. I want to ask about the place, but decide it's better to keep my mouth shut. It feels like we've wandered into a recreation of a 16th Century European village.

But what on earth is it doing in California?

He grunts and jerks his head the way he wants us to go. I walk after him, breathing in the crisp night air.

We walk for a long time in utter silence. There isn't a hint of modern technology anywhere. It's rustic and quiet and even peaceful—and I can't help the feeling that I'm missing some significant piece of the puzzle about this place.

It's the timing, I think. *There's no way it should still be night.*

We pass more darkened homes. They're well maintained, obviously not abandoned. But if people live here, shouldn't there be some sign of them? Even if it is night, there's bound to be *something*... a light from inside a window, the sounds of a family gathering at a table, heck, even a tavern or —

"Impressed yet?" Raul interrupts my thoughts.

I choose my words carefully. "What would I be impressed by?"

"The stillness," Raul breathes. "It's wonderful, isn't it?"

I look at him askance. "I'm not sure I know what you mean."

Just then, the sound of running footsteps reaches us. I turn my head immediately—and see a young, blond girl stumbling out from around a corner of the street.

She staggers to a stop and gives a cry of alarm when she sees us. She has to be my age, but her clothes… they're nothing like anyone would wear today. They are the clothes of a medieval peasant.

Before I know what is happening, Raul splits from me and catches the girl by the nape of her neck. She gasps in fear but doesn't fight back.

In fact, her entire body starts to tremble.

"April," he growls. "What are you doing out at this hour?" He twists his hand in her hair. She whimpers. "Did you not hear of the edict?"

"I… I… I…" she blubbers. I can tell she's obviously frightened. "I was… I…"

"Yes?" Raul asks. "Tell me." His voice takes on the deep baritone of a predator.

She swallows and shakes her head and squeezes her eyes shut. "Just do it," she whispers. "Punish me. Do it, but don't make me wait."

At her invitation Raul sweeps her hair away and exposes her

neck. He draws his lips back as if he's going to bite her...

"No!" I cry out. I run to them. I don't know what nightmare this is, but I won't stand by and do nothing.

I grab Raul's arm and pull him away. "Let her go!"

He throws me off him as if I weigh no more than a paper doll. I fall to the ground and grunt. Already Raul has April in his embrace. He drops her back, almost like a lover...

"Stop!" I scream. I pick myself up and throw myself at them. "Don't hurt her!"

Raul moves with astonishing speed. My effort nets me nothing but my hands grasping through empty air, in the spot they'd just been.

Raul looks from April to me. The poor girl is staring at me, wide-eyed. "You care," he says slowly, "what happens to this wench?"

I flinch at his choice of words. April gives no response. She just stands there, drained, devoid of life.

She looks like she's given up.

"Yes, I care," I say. "What were you going to do to her? Is she another one like me, caught up in this twisted game?"

Raul's lips twitch up. Maybe in a smile, maybe in a snarl —
it's hard to tell.

"Let me assure you…" he lets her go and steps toward me,
"…that this girl is nothing like you."

I try to catch her eye, but her gaze is glued to the ground.
She's free now—why doesn't she run?

Raul stops an equal distance between us. He sweeps an arm
back to take in April. "She's broken the rules," he tells me softly.
"And she knows what happens to humans who come out after
curfew. Especially on a night like this."

I start to edge my way toward them, so I can get between
Raul and April. He's already proved he's not willing to hurt me. At
least — not in the way he was ready to hurt April.

"Please," the girl says softly. "Just do what you have to. Don't
— don't stretch it out."

I have no idea if she's crazy or what. Maybe this is some type
of role-playing game gone horribly wrong.

"I would," Raul says. "But it looks like our incumbent Prin-
cess-in-waiting has other ideas for you."

I stop short. "What did you call me?"

He ignores the question. He turns back and grabs April's arm. She gives a small cry as he drags her forward and then pushes her toward me.

I catch her as she stumbles into my arms. Our eyes meet for a split-second, and I see such intense *hatred* in hers that I gasp.

She brushes me off and stands on her own.

"So, April," Raul says. "It looks like you have a new champion." He smiles. "I wonder what James will say when he finds out. That's where you were running from, isn't it? You were *with* him?"

Her cheeks flush a deep red.

Raul starts walking. "I was going to show you the majesty of The Haven," he tells me. "But this little wrinkle necessitates a change in plans. Come. Your new lodgings await."

Chapter Thirteen

ELEIRA

Raul brings me and April past the edge of the village to the mouth of a small cave. Our whole walk there I kept my eyes open, cataloguing everything I saw and planting the layout of the place into my memory.

I'll need to know where to go when I try to escape.

The cave entrance is deceptive of its interior. As we walk into the mountain, the cavern opens up to many times its size. There are torches lining the walls. Raul grabs one near the entrance and shoves it into my hands without a word.

I'm amazed how well he manages in the darkness. The fire casts only the smallest halo of light, and he is far on the outer edge of it.

As we walk, I try again and again to catch April's eyes. She, however, is completely unresponsive.

After a long time walking I hear the sound of running water. It gets louder and louder the deeper we go. The tunnel twists, then opens, and I hear the roar of a great underground river from in front of us.

I also see a line of cell doors carved into the sides.

Raul strolls up to one and opens it. He looks at us in expectation. For the second time tonight, I think his eyes somehow shine in the dark. But the illusion only lasts for a second before fading.

"Your new home," he says. "For now."

I look around for an escape, but I know if I run he'll be on me in a second. There's no way I could navigate the underground passages on my own.

So — tired, hungry, and resigned — I go into the prison cell, trailed by April.

She shoots one spiteful glare at me as she walks by and then returns to her regular docile demeanor.

Raul closes and locks the door. The clang of the metal bars shutting echoes through the space.

He turns to leave.

"Wait!" I call out. "Do you just mean to leave us here? What about food? What about water?"

"Those will be provided to you soon enough," he says.

"How long are you going to leave us here?" I demand. "Raul! Raul!"

But he has already walked away.

Not long after his footsteps fade, a snicker comes from behind me.

I turn and discover April staring daggers at me.

"Well done," she says sardonically. "Really, very spectacular. *'Don't hurt her!'*" she mocks.

Suddenly I'm angry. "What's with the attitude?" I demand. "Is that the thanks I get for saving your life?"

"Save my life?" She bursts out laughing. Then, just as quickly, she cuts off. "Sweetie, all you did was condemn me to a living hell."

"Whatever," I mutter. I grip the metal bars and try shaking them to see if they'll give.

"Don't bother," she tells me. "You're not getting out until they decide to release us."

I give the bars one more shake and realize she's right.

"Besides," she continues casually. She folds her legs and slides down to sit on the floor. "You don't want to be out there tonight. You're safest behind bars."

I shake my head. "Safe from what?"

"My, you really don't know anything, do you?" she says. There's a trace of pity in her voice. "There's a full moon tonight."

I wait for her to expand on that explanation, but she says nothing else. "So?" I ask finally.

"So?" she sounds incredulous. "So, it's the night our masters are most consumed by..." she pauses for a dramatic moment, "...the bloodlust."

My head jerks to her. "What?"

"You were wondering why you didn't see anyone else," she says. She gives a little laugh. "Why there weren't any other humans out and about? Don't worry about how I know. It's the same with all new sacrifices."

A shiver creeps down my spine. "Sacrifices?"

"Oh, yeah," she says casually. "They bring girls like you to us every few weeks. Usually when there's a... shortage."

I turn to her. "A shortage? A shortage of what?"

"Blood. Duh!" She shrugs. "Whatever. You'll figure it all out before long."

Is everyone here crazy? "Why did you just give yourself to him like that? You didn't fight back or anything."

She snorts. "As if any of us can fight back against them. Look. I'll do you a favor." She stands up and walks to me. "I don't know how long you intend to survive. But here's a hint; it's not up to you. Not at all. I was like you once. I came from the *Outside*. And I —" she stops. A frown forms on my face. "I..."

"Yes?" I ask. "You what?"

"I —" April holds a hand to her forehead. She closes her eyes and shakes her head. "I —"

Alarm sweeps through me. "Are you okay?" I ask.

"Fine," she says roughly.

"What were you saying?"

"I... I can't." She shakes her head once more. "The... I..."

Then her eyes open, and there's an absolute vacant look in them.

Without another word she simply folds down and sits cross-legged on the ground.

I run up to her despite my better judgement. I put a hand on her shoulder. "April?"

She looks at me with big, empty eyes. "Yes," she says. "That's my name." She cocks her head to one side. "I'm April. Who are you?"

"My name's Eleira," I say.

"That's a pretty name." She smiles. "I like it."

I look at her in concern. The inflection of her voice is totally different from before. She sounds like a child.

"You were saying something about the Outside?" I ask.

She gasps. "Oh no," she says. "No, no, no, no." She brings her knees to her chest and starts to rock back and forth. "Not about that. We mustn't speak about that. No. No. Never."

My body tenses. She sounds as if she's been brainwashed, or like a switch has been flipped, and reduced her into some primordial state.

But I can't just let the subject go.

"Why?" I ask her. "What's wrong with speaking about that?"

"It's... forbidden," she says. Her voice is a ghost of its former self. "I'm sorry, I can't, I..." She lies down. "I'm so tired. So very tired. I need to sleep."

She closes her eyes. Before I can say another word, she's

completely out.

I draw away. A sense of dread and fear and apprehension consume me.

What's been done to me? I shiver. *Is that also my fate?*

***

More time passes. I spend it alone with my own thoughts. They go down devious paths. April doesn't stir. About an hour in, maybe more, maybe less, the sound of slow, trudging footsteps reaches my ears.

I crawl to the bars and try to see past them. The sound is coming from deep in the caves. A few minutes later, an old woman wrapped in a dirty shawl appears from the darkness.

She's carrying a bucket in one hand and a cloth bag in the other. She approaches my cell. Without a word she sets the bucket down, about five feet away from the bars.

Then she reaches into the bag and takes out a loaf of bread.

My mouth waters.

She doesn't look at me as she dips the loaf in the bucket. It comes out coated in a white, milky substance.

She takes a few steps forward and wordlessly puts it on the ground, just out of my reach..

Then she turns around and walks away.

"Wait!" I say. "Please, wait!"

She moves on as if never having heard me.

I stick an arm through the cage and try to reach the loaf. My fingers almost brush against the surface. I contort myself lower and try to squeeze my shoulder through, I reach and strain and try to get it.

But all I manage is to push it farther away. A soft laugh comes from behind me. "Don't bother. It's just there to tempt you."

I look over. April is up. The vacancy is gone from her eyes. She sounds like the girl I first met.

"It's food," I say. "And I'm starving." I look around our cell. My eyes fall on the torch. "Quick. Give me that!"

"Ugh." She rolls her eyes. "That's not a good idea."

I mutter something unpleasant under my breath and retrieve the torch myself. I lift it from its place on the wall. I start waving it around to put the fire out, but then realize if I do, we'd be bathed in total darkness.

So instead I go back to the gate and stick it through, fire and all. I use it to nudge the loaf closer. A spark of excitement lights inside me as it skids within reach.

I grab it and quickly rip it in two. I offer one half to April.

She shakes her head. "No thanks."

"Suit yourself." I'm just about to put it into my mouth when another thought hits me. "Is it poisoned?"

"Hah!" she laughs. "No. If they wanted you dead they have other ways of doing it."

I'm not completely assured by her words. I sniff the piece in my hand. "What's this white stuff?"

She shrugs. "Probably goat's milk."

"Spoiled?"

"Does it smell spoiled?"

"No."

"Then no." She sees me still hesitate. She exhales, and takes the free half. She bites into it, chews, and swallows.

"See?" she says. "It's safe."

A ravenous hunger takes me. I wolf my half down. April hands me hers, and I have that as well.

"So," I say when I'm done. "Are we on speaking terms now? Can you tell me what this place is?"

"You know what it is," she tells me. "You're in The Haven. These —" she gestures grandly around her, "— are The Catacombs. It's where they keep the humans when we can't be above ground."

"You keep saying 'they.' You call them the masters," I shudder. "Why?"

"That's who they are. They rule this place. If you stay quiet and meek, you might survive. But," she gives a bitter laugh, "you've ruined all chances of that for me."

"How?" I say. "By protecting you?" My annoyance with her is growing. "I *stopped* Raul from killing you!"

"He wouldn't have killed me!" she exclaims. They don't *kill* anybody, except on a night like tonight."

As if on cue, distant screams come from far away.

I spin to the entrance. "What was that?"

She smiles at me softly. "The sounds of the sacrifices, taken out of their pens." She gives me a hard look. "You better get used to it." She settles down. "It's going to be going on for *hours.*"

Chapter Fourteen

RAUL

I watch the commotion far below me from the balcony of my tower.

The humans — those deemed weak, frail, sick, and useless — have been released into the night. They huddle together as one big group in the midst of the clearing.

I can smell their fright. I can sense their terror. They all know what's about to happen. They know the rules, and they know their lives have all been forfeit.

I look past them, at the surrounding trees. The dark shapes of my coven's vampires shift and move there. They're anxious, too. With the full moon out tonight, it's all they can do to control their thirst.

"If we didn't do this, they'd rip *all* the humans to shreds."

I turn my head. Phillip is sitting in a lotus pose against the glass door to my room. His eyes are closed, his body absolutely still.

"I know," I grunt. My hands grip the railing. "But it doesn't mean there isn't a better way."

"As long as Mother rules…"

"Yes, yes, I know." My eyes return to the herd of humans. I see James's distinctive figure stroll into their midst.

A wide space opens up before him. They're all terrified.

He raises his arms, and a hush falls. He smiles, holds his head high, and conducts one slow circle.

The vampires around the edge of the woods are chomping at the bit to be released. But they know, as well as I do, that there is ceremony that must be adhered to.

"Citizens of The Haven," James announces. "Welcome. It warms my heart that so many of you have chosen to join us tonight."

"Does he have to mock them?" I grumble under my breath.

"You all know the rules of the game." James laughs. "On my count, you will be given a head start to run and hide anywhere you please. My friends in the woods —" he gestures to the dark trees, "— will afford you the privilege of *time*, before coming after you. How much time, you ask? Why —" his voice takes a triumphant tone, "— however much time *I* deem appropriate. This night, I'm in a particularly indulgent mood. Because, as some of you might already know..." he walks to the circle of trees and addresses our kin, "...I've been sent away by our most glorious Queen on a mission of immense importance. From this night forth, until my triumphant return, it is my brother who will oversee The Hunt!"

He spins and points a finger right at me. I curse and start to step away, but Phillip's sudden hand on my shoulder keeps me in place.

"The others are watching," he says softly. "Don't let them see any weakness."

I know he's right. I grit my teeth and force a stiff smile.

James turns back and speaks to the humans. "Remember, too, that this is a competition. You may use all means to get ahead. Whatever you think might give you an advantage..." he bends down and scoops up a rock, "...you are free to use."

He hefts the stone in his hand, taking aim, and throws it at the gong half a field away.

"GO!" he yells as it strikes. "The last human standing receives the gift of eternal life! RUN!"

And just like that, the people scatter. They go in all directions, oblivious to how many vampires are waiting for them in the woods.

And when the last of the humans disperse into the trees... the screaming starts.

Chapter Fifteen

RAUL

"Eternal life?" I glare at James, hardly able to contain my anger. "You promised them *eternal* life?"

"A joke," he says casually. He takes his wineglass from the table and swirls it around.

It's filled with the blood of the last surviving human from The Hunt.

"I thought it would give them a little extra motivation," he continues. "And boy, does the blood of one filled with hope taste sweet."

"You lied to them," I snarl.

He laughs, "So? This is *our* kingdom, brother." He leans toward me. "What's life without a little bit of fun?"

"Do you forget," I say hastily, "that we need to coexist with humans? That we *depend* on them to survive? What would happen if word gets out of your promise? And if they know you reneged on it —"

"Blah, blah, blah," he mocks. "Who's going to tell them? How are they going to find out?"

"The other vampires talk —"

"And you think any of them would be fools enough to let that slip? My, Raul, but you have a poor opinion of our kind."

"It's not that," I say. How can I explain to James what I really mean? There's a difference between ruling as a hated autocrat and ruling with the respect of your subjects. No matter who we are, or what our true nature is...

James stands, "You've always been a dreamer," he tells me. "But you are impetuous, too, like me. Don't think I'm blind to our similarities, little brother. You want... adoration. You want to be seen and respected and adored. But, guess what?" He steps behind me and brings his lips to my ear. "You will never have the respect of humans. We, all of us, are monsters to their eyes. And who can ever love a monster, except one who is equally... *evil?*"

I shake my head roughly. *Liana loved me, and I let her go.*

I shift the subject away from me. "Do you remember the last rebellion? Do you understand that the humans outnumber us in The Haven ten-to-one?"

"Rebellion?" He sneers. "More like an eradication."

"No," I say. "We were almost overthrown."

"Don't be ridiculous. As if they ever posed a real threat."

"They poisoned their blood without us knowing," I remind him. "We almost didn't catch on before it was too late."

"But we did catch on, didn't we?" he says. "Mother saw right through their little scheme. Besides. That was what, three, four centuries ago? I *highly* doubt the knowledge of how to do it remains with them."

James is missing the point completely. "Thousands died," I say. "It took us decades to rebuild what we lost. If one of the other covens attacked when we were vulnerable..." I steady my gaze. "The Haven wouldn't exist today."

"And I guess that's why Mother is sending me on this diplomatic mission," James says. "Right in time for the succession. You know, I've come around to the idea of it, after all."

I scoff in disbelief. "Is that so?"

"As a matter of fact, it is. The way I see it, the greatest threat comes from the Outside. Father's coven is strongest, but, cut off the head of the snake and his empire will crumble. Even better, *little* brother, who stands next in line to succeed in The Crypts?"

I look at him in disbelief. "Are you implying that... no." I break out laughing. "You think... you think they will accept *you* as their leader? Please!"

"And why not?" James flares back and pulls himself to full height. "His blood flows in my veins. I have an ability you never did. I can see past the surface. I can decipher the meaning hidden behind Mother's words. And isn't it extraordinarily obvious? She sent me to *unite* the covens. Together... we will be unstoppable. Our kind will rule the world! None shall stand in our way."

A tingle of fear creeps up my back. "What you're talking about is... exposure." I breathe. "It goes against everything we've ever worked for!"

"Oh, Raul, how you disappoint me. I am so tired to hiding. Aren't you? The Haven is so... claustrophobic. There's an entire world out there. Why must our kind linger in the shadows while humans, while the weaker species, go out and have it all? Tell me!"

"This is madness," I breathe. "Listen to yourself —"

"No *you* listen!" he interrupts.

"Lestat had it right —"

"Lestat was a fiction!"

"No," James growls. "Let our kind be known! Let our kind be celebrated! Let the humans come, with their guns blazing, and just *try* to take us on! They are beneath us, all of them. The life we lead now has no prosperity. Why, it's no life at all! I say, let us make right what is ours! Let's claim the world. We have as much right to it as they do!"

"No," I say. "No, you're wrong. The world is not made for us. We are creatures of darkness. Sun, the light — it is our scourge."

"And why must days be defined by when the sun shines?" he asks. "The world is bathed in night for an equal amount of time. We will flip civilization on its head!"

"You forget," I snarl, "How much the world outside has changed. We keep our people locked in time in the sixteenth century! Superstition and fear rule their hearts. But out there, James... we wouldn't stand a chance."

He laughs. "That is simply a difference of opinion."

"Our people are meek," I stress. "We've raised them to be so. Outside, they have weapons — real weapons that they can use against us. You think a stake through the heart is bad? Wait until they capture one of our kind and get us into their labs. They'll dissect every bit of blood — every strand of DNA. They'll discover weaknesses even we don't know we have! The illusion of safety Mother has maintained has made you arrogant. When the entire human race rises up against us, you think we will survive?"

"You do *not?*" James hisses. "You make me sick. We are the predators. We are the hunters." He gestures roughly out in front of him. "The world out there is ripe for the plucking. It's inhabited by cowards and sheep! We are the wolves, dear brother. And *we* are the ones destined to rule."

Chapter Sixteen

ELEIRA

Even though it's been quiet for hours, I can't get the last of the screams out of my head.

I've never heard such blood-curdling sounds. They, and the memory of them, confirm to me — if nothing else does — that whatever this situation is, it's real. It's real, and it's very, very dangerous.

"How much longer are they going to keep us here?"

April shrugs in apathy. "Who knows?"

"I can't believe you can just take it," I say. "Don't you want to run? To escape?"

"Escape?" April's voice rises in surprise. "No, no. You don't understand. Once you're inside The Haven, there *is* no escape." She looks at the ceiling. "The only escape from here is death."

My eyes narrow. "How can you be so defeatist?"

"It's called reality," she says. She turns her shoulder to me, indicating the conversation is over.

But I won't give up that easily. I walk to her and crouch down to her level.

"Please," I say. "There must be something you know. You say you came from the Outside. That means you're like me, doesn't it? That means you —"

April starts shaking her head, over and over and over again, almost obsessively, as soon as she hears the word *Outside*.

"No, no no, no no no," she repeats. "I can't say. No. No, no."

"Okay okay okay," I say quickly trying to calm her. "I won't mention the Out—" I swallow the trigger word before I can set her off again. "We won't talk about your past. Okay?"

Her muttering slows down, and then she nods. "Yes," she says. "That is a good idea."

I bite my lip, thinking of the best way to approach the subject.

"April," I say her name firmly. I take her by the shoulders and look into her eyes. "I want you to tell me everything you know about The Haven. Can you do that?"

She looks at me suspiciously. "You're very persistent. Why?"

"I have to know what we're dealing with." The shock of waking up in that strange room, then being brought here has worn off to the point that I now think I'm capable of making plans. "The creatures holding us here. They're... what?"

"Vampires," she says.

I swallow. I don't want to believe that's true, but for now, what choice do I have?

"And you said tonight they were... I mean, all the screams..."

"They were feeding," she says. "Killing." She nods. "It's a way of life."

"Raul... when he found you..."

"He was going to feed, too."

"And I stopped him?"

"Yes." She shakes her head. "I still don't understand how you were able to do that."

Neither do I, I think.

"He said there was an edict. What did he mean?"

"The Haven becomes a killing ground every full moon," she tells me. "There's a lottery that selects the... contestants... for The

Hunt. Everybody's name is put in. But the weak have the odds titled heavily in their favor. Whoever gets drawn, that's who is sacrificed.

"They crowd the people outside. When the gong goes, the vampires are let loose. It becomes every man for himself."

My gut clenches. "That's horrible," I say.

April shrugs again. "As I said, it's the way of life around here."

A clatter behind us makes me spin around. An unfamiliar man in a red coat is standing on the other side of the bars, staring at us with raw hunger in his eyes.

April's breath catches. "Oh no," she gulps.

"What?" I say. My head jerks from her to him. "What is it? What?"

"It's one of The Convicted," she says. Pure terror fills her words.

The pale man's hands grip the bars. His mouth opens. My eyes go wide when I see his gums. He has no teeth — none, aside from two long fangs glistening at the front.

"Don't move," April hisses. "There's a chance that maybe —"

He emits a low, awful moan.

It's such a painful sound that my hands clamp up and cover my ears. I cry out. I can't help it. The moan makes it feel like my brain is being crushed within my skull.

Those starved eyes latch onto me. April curses. "He's seen you!"

Before I can do anything, the man lunges down and throws an arm through the bars. Frigid fingers wrap around my ankle. I scream and kick at him. But the grip is unwavering. He pulls me to him.

I skid across the floor. I jerk and writhe and try to break free, but it's no use. A bone-chilling cold comes over me, originating from his grip. My muscles start to seize up. His fangs shine cruelly, coated with spit.

Just when I'm about to be made into a meal, two hands grab my shoulders. My head swings up. I see April pulling back with all her might.

"Don't just freeze!" she yells at me. "Fight him! Resist!"

Her spark ignites something in me. I start to kick again. The Convicted moans, and the sound is horrible.

He's stronger than both of us. April's effort may have granted me a few extra seconds, but no more. She digs her heels in and pulls me back, yet all she achieves is stretching out the time before the inevitable.

Suddenly, the man gives a mammoth roar and jerks my leg through the bars. I'm yanked out of April's grasp. She cries out and falls.

His dead eyes light up in glee. He widens his jaw, and is just about to clamp those fangs into my leg like a shark...

A black shape moves behind him. I only get the barest hint of warning before the grip on my leg slackens. I kick free, confusion rolling through me. Why did he stop?

Then I see the gruesome sight in front of me. There's a hand sticking out through The Convicted's chest. In it is his bloodied heart.

Suddenly, the hand closes, crushing the heart. The man in the red jacket croaks and crumbles down. And behind him, I see the dark shape emerge as none other than Raul.

Chapter Seventeen

RAUL

I pull back from the disgusting creature who's now dead at my feet.

All sorts of questions flare through my mind. How did he get free? How did he find Eleira and April? And worst of all, what would have happened had I not decided to come back for them just now?

I scramble to open the cell door. Eleira staggers away from me. She's breathing hard, and her eyes are wide in terror.

"You... you killed him," she gasps. "With your bare hands! *How?*"

I look down at my bloody hand and grimace in disgust. I wipe it clean on The Convicted's shirt.

April's recovered herself enough to give a small laugh. "You saw how," she tells the other girl.

I look at both of them. "Leaving you here was a mistake," I

say. "April, I'm sending you back to your family. Eleira — you're coming with me."

She shakes her head. She's obviously in shock. "No," she says. "No, I'm not —"

I grab her arm. "You think you're safer on your own?" I hiss. "You have enemies you don't even know about." That's the only explanation I can come up with to make sense of The Convicted's presence.

I stab a finger at her. "Do you think that was just coincidence? I should never have left you alone."

"What do you *want* from me?" she asks. Her voice trembles. "What is this world you've brought me into?"

April stares at me in defiance. "I am *not* going back to my 'family!'" she exclaims.

"Fine," I snarl. "Then stay here." I pull Eleira with me. "You and I are leaving."

She breaks free. "Not without April!"

I can almost roll my eyes in exasperation. "I'm not here for some teen drama," I say. "You are my *prisoner*," I spit at her. "In case you haven't noticed. And you, April, have absolutely no say in this. I don't even know why I'm entertaining this conversation with you two."

I stare toward the entrance and hold the cage door open. "You want to know what this world is? Then come with me now."

Eleira looks from me to April. She looks at the body of The Convicted on the ground.

Finally, she swallows and nods. She walks grudgingly to me.

"Good girl," I say. She shoots me a glare.

April remains in the far reaches of the cell. "If you're sending me back to *them*," she begins.

"James is gone," I tell her roughly. "If you think he's going to come down and rescue you..." I bark a laugh. "We both know what you are to him. Don't deceive yourself into thinking you're something more."

Eleira takes in our conversation. A fleck of understanding shows in her eyes. Wisely, she keeps her mouth shut.

"You don't *know* what James and I have," April begins.

"Really?" It almost saddens me, her naivety. "My brother left The Haven after The Hunt. He won't be back for weeks. Maybe months."

April takes a sharp breath. Obviously, that's news to her.

"That's the choice I'm giving you," I say. "Go back to your family, or stay here. Who knows how long you'll be down here before somebody finds you."

Eleira's eyes widen. Quickly, she runs back to the other girl. She grabs her hand and whispers something in her ear. I can eavesdrop by tuning my hearing in to them, but I choose not to.

I don't need to be more aware of Eleira than I already am. It's already taking every bit of self-control I have to restrain myself around her.

Of course, the stench of The Convicted's corpse helps a great deal in shielding me from Eleira's sweet smell.

After a heavy series of back and forth whispers, both girls approach, holding hands.

Eleira straightens and looks right at me. "I'll only go with you *willingly*," she says. "If I get to keep April with me. I don't know much about this place, but *she* does. And since you're not very forthcoming, I'll need to rely on someone I trust as a guide."

My eyebrows slowly creep up at her little speech.

"It's been a long time since anyone's made demands of me." I shake my head and laugh softly. "But if that's what you want... fine. Just be warned, you're not doing April any favors."

That only strengthens Eleira's resolve. "She's coming with us."

"Then let's go."

Chapter Eighteen

ELEIRA

I trail after Raul, holding April's hand.

He's led us out of The Catacombs and back above ground. It's still night. It's still dark.

That makes me uneasy. It feels as if we're trapped in time.

But I've already come to terms that nothing about this place is natural. If I'm going to escape, I have to put aside any preconceived notions about what is and what isn't possible, about what is and what isn't real.

Because, very clearly, my understanding of the world is severely lacking if creatures like the one walking in front of me exist.

"The rest of us — the rest of the humans — are going to be coming back soon," April whispers in my ear. "They lead their lives above ground, in the village." She casts a look at the empty buildings and huts around us. "During The Hunt, they go to the caves for safety. After, they all return to their lives."

I nod slowly, starting to understand at least a *bit* of how The Haven works.

"You call them 'they,'" I say. "Not 'us,' Why?"

"Because I'm from the Out —" she stops. "The Out —" She frowns, as if she can't get the word out. "I'm from —"

"It's okay," I tell her. I squeeze her hand. "I understand."

She frowns. "Do you? Because I don't."

I'm not sure if she's sincere or not. That, in and of itself, is quite frightening.

How do you brainwash someone to stop them from being able to acknowledge their past?

Raul stops in front of a massive redwood. He runs a hand over the trunk. Two pieces peel away as if by magic, and the steel doors of an elevator reveal themselves to us.

"We're going up," he says. "You need to leave her here."

"What?" I look at April. "You promised —"

My words die in my throat when I see April's face. Her expression has gone slack again. That eerie vacancy is right back in her eyes.

She stares at the tree trunk without seeing.

Raul emits an annoyed grunt. He turns and passes a hand up and down over April's eyes.

She remains unreactive.

"She's bewitched," he explains. "She can't see the same thing you and I can."

"What? What do you mean?"

"*All* the villagers are like that," Raul says. "You can thank the Queen for that. Any mention of life outside of what they're allowed to know, any hint that there's something *more* going on beyond their walls... and they turn into that."

"Zombies," I breathe, aghast and disgusted and saddened and repelled.

"No," Raul shakes his head. "She'll snap out of it when the elevator doors are hidden. A real zombie is the creature who attacked you."

I shudder at that memory. "Who *was* he?"

"A vampire who broke the law," Raul says. His lips curl up, and he flashes me a peculiar smile. "You see? I can explain things to you as well. Even better than your appointed guide. Now come on." He jerks his hand to the elevator. "We need to go."

"But April —"

"Will be perfectly safe here. See that?" he points toward a nearby hut. "It's her home." He points at another one. "So is that one. And that one. She's welcome, she's *safe*, anywhere. But the same cannot be said about you. So let's go, before more of the humans discover you're here."

His tone leaves no room for argument. I try to give April a tug but she remains unmoving.

"You're wasting your time," Raul says from inside the elevator.

I sigh and let April go. I walk into the elevator, of my own free will—with a vampire.

The thought is staggering.

The doors close, and we reach the top. I go to the railing to check for April.

She's already gone.

I turn on Raul. "Why would it matter if the other humans know I'm here?" I ask.

"Isn't it obvious?" He steps toward me and reaches up to

brush my neck.

I draw a short breath. He's so close. My heart starts thundering.

He drops his voice. He doesn't look me in the eyes, instead focusing on that spot where I found the strange mark. "You've been bitten," he says. "And you're still alive." A smile forms on his lips. The proximity of his body makes all sorts of inappropriate images flash through my mind. Inappropriate because of who he is, and who I am, and what our relationship is to one another.

What would it feel like to have his lips on mine?

Whoa! Where did that thought come from?

"They'd hate you," he continues softly, glazing his fingers over my neck, while I stand there, struck dumb and unable to move. "For the same reason that I would adore you. You're in the process... of being turned."

Then, just as suddenly, he steps away. The gulf of space between us makes me sway on unsteady feet.

"But you're not there yet," he tells me. "And you won't be there for a long time. Now come. I want to show you the room you can expect to be yours should you prove willing to accept your fate."

My mind grapples with the new information I've been given.

"I'm being turned?" I say. The words feel so ludicrous to say out loud. "Why? How? I mean—vampires aren't real," I swallow. "Right?"

I shake my head. I'm alone in the enormous room Raul brought me to. There's a circular bed in the middle of the room. Beautiful, sillton blue sheets adorn it. There's a glass door leading to a balcony from where I can see the whole village beneath me. But, the weird thing is, when Raul and April and I walked through the streets below, and I looked up, I could not see the balcony. All I saw were the thick branches and stars.

And if that's not enough for me to question my sanity, I'm now talking to myself in the mirror.

I brush my hair back and look at my neck. There's nothing there anymore. I run my hands along the smooth skin. Nothing at all to give evidence to the bump I woke up with, or the two small bite marks.

I wander to the bed and sit down. The mattress is firm. Everything about this particular room is the epitome of luxury.

Why would they bring me to a cell beneath the earth and then put me up in something like this? Is it just to mess with my mind?

Whatever the goal is — it's working. I've never felt more confused or off-balance than I do now. And to top it off, I have to deal with my budding attraction to one very handsome, very *dangerous*, flame-haired man.

Flame-haired vampire?

I try to think of all I know about the supernatural and mythical. But my knowledge is woefully lacking. After the experience in the woods with Michael, it's like my mind shut off from anything that could not be explained scientifically. I became drawn to concrete subjects in school — math and history and the hard sciences. That's how I ended up skipping a year ahead and being one year younger than all my peers at university. It's why I was the only seventeen-year-old to matriculate at my class at Stanford.

It's why I'm probably the worst-prepared person in the world to deal with what I'm seeing around me now.

The door to my room opens. I look up.

A beautiful woman flows in. She's adorned in a stunning white gown that hugs her figure and emphasizes every feminine curve. She can't be more than a few years older than me, but the way she carries herself makes me feel immediately self-conscious.

I start to stand. She flutters a hand at me. "Please, don't trouble yourself."

Even her voice is beautiful.

I sit back down, my spine rigid. "Who are you?" I ask.

She smiles. "My name is Morgan," she tells me. She waits for my reaction. When I give none, she winks. "And you must be Eleira. It's wonderful to finally meet you."

She glides across the room and gently lowers herself onto a free seat.

I shift uncomfortably. She's completely at home here, whereas I am still as jumpy as a cat stranded on a raft in a pond.

She has dark eyes that shine with intelligence. "I hope you've enjoyed your stay so far," she tells me. "Every effort has been made to accommodate your arrival."

"Are you going to tell me what's going on?" I ask. "Raul says

—"

"Oh, so you've met my son."

I gawk at her. "Your *son?*" I shake my head. "That's — that's not possible."

She laughs lightly. Her voice is like chiming bells. "I'll take that as a compliment of my youth," she tells me. She catches her reflection in the mirror and smiles her perfect smile. "Raul is my son. One of three boys. I believe you've met the others... no?" She frowns. "Maybe not yet. You will, soon enough. I'll make sure you're *all* acquainted. After all, we have a wedding to plan."

"Excuse me?" None of this is making any sense. "A wedding? Whose?"

"Yours, of course, sweet girl. Do you think just anybody can wander into The Haven from the outside world?" She shakes her head. "No, no. You are privileged, my dear. Because of the circumstances of your birth, you've been granted nearly unprecedented power... and influence... over all our lives." She smiles again. "I know you're confused, but everything will make sense before long."

She stands and walks toward me. She stops in front of me and cups my face in her hands. "My, but you are a beauty, aren't you?" she asks. "We'll have to do something about that awful out-fit, though. Oh, I know." She snaps her fingers, and the doors of the wardrobe fly open. "You'll find everything to your heart's desire in there. Next time I see you, I expect you to be dressed as one befitting your position."

And then, without another word, she simply gets up and leaves the room.

My shock only lasts a moment. I run to the doors after her and rattle the handles.

Just as before, they're locked.

I grunt. *Wedding?* I think. *What on earth is she talking about, I'm not getting married.*

It seems like every conversation I have reveals more to me but lends confusion rather than clarity.

I turn my attention to the wardrobe. How did she open it like that?

The fabrics inside catch my eye. There are an assortment of dresses hanging there.

All of them look just as extravagant as hers.

I walk over and run a hand over them. Despite myself, I get

goosebumps. I've never imagined feeling anything this expensive against my skin.

Is this really right? I wonder. Only an hour ago I saw somebody get killed. And now I'm entertaining the notion of putting on clothes picked out for me?

All this is totally insane.

But there's nothing to be done about it. I pick out a light blue dress and hold it up before me in front of a mirror. I stroke the material. It's wonderfully soft and looks to be *exactly* my size.

No, I shake my head. This is ridiculous. I'm not going to put *their* clothes on. No way, no how.

Yet after half an hour, my resolve fades. I'm cooped up in these chambers with nothing else to do.

I sigh and strip out of the clothes linking me to my previous life. No sooner do I have the first dress on that a soft tapping comes from the door.

I spin around. The door creeps open, and a meek-looking serving girl comes in.

"I was asked to see if you require anything," she says. Her eyes are downcast and her voice is barely above a whisper. "If you're hungry, I can—"

"Yes!" I say. The girl flinches. Is she scared of me? "I mean, yes, please, that would be wonderful." The last meal I had scarcely made a dent in my hunger.

She bows and starts out the room.

"Hold on," I say. "What's your name?"

She gives a little gasp of surprise. "I'm…" she begins. My ears perk up.

"…Unable to tell you," she finished lamely.

I narrow my eyes. "Why?"

"I'm sorry," she says. "The less we speak, the better it is. For me. You understand?"

Not really, I want to say. Instead, I exhale. "Of course."

She draws back. Just before she leaves, she adds, very softly, "You have stunning eyes, Princess."

Princess?

Chapter Nineteen

RAUL

"She's quite a jewel," Mother says as she walks through the palace. "You are lucky to have her."

I follow in her stead with my hands clasped behind my back. I don't have to voice my discomfort with the whole situation. Once the Queen makes up her mind, there's little that can be said to dissuade her.

"I doubt she feels the same about me," I tell her stiffly.

She laughs. "Oh, nonsense." She bends by a vase of flowers and inhales deeply. "These smell lovely. Who chose them?"

"I don't know." My voice is tinged with annoyance. "How can you think about frivolities like that now, Mother?"

She clicks her tongue and moves on. "You know I don't like you calling me that." She sighs. "Alas, it is something I will have to get used to, won't I?"

"As if you haven't in the past centuries?"

She gives me a sharp look.

I rake a hand through my hair. "I'm sorry. I speak to you without thinking."

"You seem to be doing a lot of that recently," she notes. "Oh well. It is of small significance. I'm sure it's something your wife will soon help correct."

I cough. "Wife?"

"Yes, of course. You're to wed the girl as soon as possible." She flows onward without looking at my reaction. "It's only prudent that we bring her into our family before the succession can truly begin. Don't you think?"

"No, I do not think, *Mother*." I stride forward and grab her arm. I turn her to face me.

She frowns at my point of contact. "Forgetting yourself again, my son?" she asks softly. "Or..." she runs a finger down my chest. "Maybe you've decided to take me up on my long-standing offer, hmm?"

I grimace and jerk my hand away. "Never."

"A pity."

"I am *not* marrying her."

Morgan laughs. "Why? Does she repel you so?"

Just the opposite, I think.

But I cannot tell the Queen that.

"It's improper," I say. "We've kidnapped her and stolen her from her life. How do you think she'll react to your proposition?"

"As a future Princess should. With dignity and grace. Remember, Raul." She touches my chest and gives a pitying look. "The ancestral blood that flows through her veins gives her the powers of the old clan of witches."

"You're telling me she is related to you?" My throat clenches. "Why am I only learning of this now? The celestial charts showed nothing of the sort!"

"No, no," Mother laughs. "Eleira comes from an entirely different line. You *do* know precious little about how it all works, don't you?"

"Being stuck with the vampire curse is enough. I don't make it a priority to learn about your kind, too."

"Something that we'll also have to change, before long, if you're to rule."

"I have no desire for —"

"Your *desires* have nothing to do with anything," she cuts in. "But I'll give you a small history lesson to broaden your knowledge. At the origin, there were five great families, all part of the witch clan. All had enormous power. Little by little, over the years, that power whittled away. Until there were only *two.* Two daughters of the clans, bound by loyalty and oath. Myself —" she raises a finger, "— and one other.

"We were both witches. Our abilities were similar, but our ambitions... were not. *She* was happy to lead a normal, disgustingly short, human life. Whereas *I* —" she stands taller, "— always aspired to something much greater. So this curse *you* always complain about — why do you not see it as I do? It is the most wonderful blessing. It is eternal life."

"It is a life of darkness."

"Perhaps. But better to have infinite nights than a limited span of days."

"I disagree."

"I know you do, sweet child." She gives me a sad look. "Your perspective is flawed. Anyway. At the time I caught wind of a little rumor... a sorcerer working at something I greatly craved. Of course —" she gives another little laugh, "— you can imagine how the story goes. The man I found was no sorcerer. But he was a vampire. And he became, in time, your father."

I stand very still, careful not to interrupt. Morgan had never shared this story with me before. As far as I know, she's never shared it with *anyone* before.

"My friend was outraged by what I'd done. She swore that my new powers would bring me nothing but misery and prophesied a horrible end. But —" she smiles, and looks at her nails, "— look at which of us is alive today and which is not."

She laughs. "Eleira is her final descendent. That is what makes her so vital to us. The abilities of witches do not flow from generation to generation. They lie latent for decades, even centuries, before one such as her is born.

"You know why I care for her? You know how important our task is? With Eleira in hand, with her on our side, with her blood joined together with yours, there are none who can ever threaten us. The two remaining lines of the great families, of the great witches, will finally be joined together as one. Can you think of any better insurance for the future?" She twirls around, oblivious in her happiness. "Because I cannot."

"You expect her to just go along with it?" I ask. "What if she resists?"

"Oh, we have many ways of breaking her, don't you worry."

"You're making her into your pawn," I say.

"For now," Morgan admits. "Eventually, she will come around. And it's not my pawn she's going to be, my son, my sweetest." She looks deep into my eyes. "It's yours."

Chapter Twenty

ELEIRA

I fell asleep after my meal. When I awoke hours later, it was still night outside.

I rose and discovered my clothes missing. Somebody must have come in and taken them.

That thought does not sit well with me. It could have been the servant girl. It could have been one of the vampires.

Who knows what *else* they could have done to me while I was so defenseless?

Suddenly, on a bout of hysteria, I laugh. *I'm* concerned about vampires taking advantage of me, just because I was asleep?

"You're their prisoner, Eleira," I mutter. "They can do anything they want to you, asleep or not."

Now *that* is a distressing thought.

I walk to the window of the balcony — my only link to the outside world. I'm surprised when I find activity in the village below. Torches are lit at regular intervals along the houses, providing a semblance of light. Amongst them, people wander to and fro, most running some sort of errands. They look like farmers, artisans, peasants. It's like I've opened up the pages of a history book and glimpsed inside. None of the people down there show any signs of belonging to this century — or the one before.

I shiver. Even though it's no longer cold, I have this feeling of being trapped in time.

The doors come open. I spin around.

Raul walks in.

He throws himself on top of a chaise and drapes one arm over its back. He hasn't seen me. But when he looks, he lets out an audible gasp.

"What?" I say.

"That dress — where did you get it?"

Is he *angry?* He certainly doesn't sound pleased.

"Um," I hesitate.

He bolts up. His eyes narrow, and for once, he looks *right* at me.

Butterflies explode in my stomach.

"Was James here?" he demands. "Is this his idea of a joke?" He takes a looming step forward. "If he was —"

"No!" I quickly say. Raul advances until I'm backed up into a corner. I try to match his eye contact, but it's impossible. His gaze is so intense, his focus is so much on me, that it makes my heart skip every other beat.

"Don't lie to me, Eleira," he says. His arms jut out. Suddenly, I'm boxed in. The proximity of his body, the heat of his glare... all of it serves to elicit some *very* intense reaction inside me.

My breathing picks up. My chest rises and falls. I'm flustered and immediately thrown off guard by this man, and it has nothing to do with *what* he is.

It's just my body's natural reaction to his very male presence.

"I'm not lying," I manage. The way he's looking at me, I'm not sure if he wants to kiss me or suck my blood.

He scowls. "Then where did you get it?"

I point a shaking finger at the wardrobe, now closed.

Raul spins off. I suck in a relieved breath.

But what's up with the strange disappointment I feel about

him leaving?

He walks to the wardrobe and flings it open. The inside is empty.

I gasp.

He turns his head, and again his piercing gaze roots me in place.

"It... it was full before," I stutter.

"I'm sure." He slams the doors with too much force. He's doing a good job containing his emotions, but I can tell that I'm walking a very thin line between peace and setting him off. And I didn't even do anything other than put on a dress.

My mind scrambles for the right thing to say. "A woman," I tell him. "A woman came in." Damn, why am I so *flustered?* "She said her name was Morgan. She told me to change into —"

I don't get to finish, because the next moment, Raul is right on me, holding me by both arms against the wall.

His strength and speed is astounding. I should be terrified, but for some reason, I'm not.

I'm just confused.

"You met the Queen?" he rasps. "She saw you? *Here?*"

I bite my lip and nod quickly. "I didn't know who she was," I say.

Raul exhales. His hands fall. But he doesn't step away.

"I'm sorry I got angry with you," he says. "But you — you don't understand. The things you do to me... the torture it is to be this close..." he brings a hand up and softly brushes my jawline.

It's the tenderest caress I've ever received in my life. It makes goosebumps explode all over my body.

"...to be so close, and to be unable to do anything about it," he finishes.

He shifts his gaze to my neck. I stand completely frozen as he focuses on the spot. He sweeps my hair away, exposing the tender expanse of skin.

"James..." he murmurs. "I can't believe James was the one to take you. How did he resist? How did he not drain you whole? Oh, Eleira, if you only knew how much I crave to be..."

He catches himself in the soliloquy and stops. His eyes widen. He looks shocked to have said so much.

As fast as ever, he rips away. He's in the center of the room before I can blink.

"I'm sorry," he says. "I shouldn't —" he swallows. "I shouldn't say such things. They'll only frighten you."

Is that... *remorse*... in his voice? I'm astounded. Here I was, this whole time seeing him as nothing more than a veritable monster...

But he isn't. He has some very human emotions running through him.

Doesn't he?

I don't know what compels me to push off from the wall and walk toward him. I don't know what it is that makes me reach out and take his hand.

I don't know what it is that makes me bring that hand to my cheek and lean against it.

"You saved me in The Catacombs," I say softly. "You shouldn't be apologizing. If anything, I should be thanking you."

Raul looks at me. His Adam's apple bobs as he swallows hard.

His hand is cold against my face. Still I keep it there, savoring the strange moment of connection. Grasping for the tiniest sense of intimacy in a place that is so foreign and scary, and yet, somehow... *magical.*

Raul twists his body toward me. He steps forward so our torsos are touching again.

I have no idea what's gotten into me. All I know is that the blossoming feelings inside are nothing I can fight.

Am I really falling for my captor?

"You're not going to kill me," I say. "Are you?"

"Eleira." He says my name with the conviction of a long-lost lover. "No. Of course not. Never. You are mine...forever ...to protect."

And then, ever so slowly, haltingly, hesitantly, he leans his head down and presses his lips to mine.

It's the lightest touch. And it only lasts a flicker of a moment. But it's enough for me to know that what he says is the absolute truth.

A spark lights in my body. Before I can respond to the chaste kiss, Raul pulls back.

Is he so timid? I think. But then I see the way his hands are shaking and the tight rigidness of his entire body.

And I realize: it must take everything he has not to devour

me right now.

He steps away. "We shouldn't do that," he says. "We shouldn't..."

But his words trail off and his eyes run once more over my body. I can see the desire burning inside him.

It's mirrored by the heavy need coursing through me.

A bolt of alarm hits me. I gasp and turn away. Have I gone totally insane? Sharing a kiss with a vampire, letting my emotions get the better of me and make me forget everything about how and why I ended up in this situation in the first place?

"No," I say. "You're right. We should *not.*"

I think I hear him sigh, but it might just be my imagination. I stare out the window into the eternal night. A part of me still believes this is one crazy dream, and I'll soon wake up and find myself back in the library, where I fell asleep...

But I know that to be the childish, irrational part. Because, crazy as all this is, I can no longer deny that The Haven is my new reality.

"Why doesn't the sun ever shine?"

"To protect us. The Queen casts spells..." Raul searches for the right words.

"I understand," I say. "What you said before?" I begin. My hands clench into fists. Tears threaten to spill from my eyes. "About me being turned. Is that true?"

There is no hesitation in his reply. "Yes."

"That means I can't go back. Can I?"

"To your old life? No. Never."

Sadness swells inside me, but the words do not come as a shock. That's pretty much what I've been expecting this whole time.

A lone tear leaks down my cheek. "Why me?" I ask.

"Because of who you are."

"Yes, but *why?*" I insist. I spin back to face him. "Morgan said there's going to be a wedding. The serving girl called me 'Princess.' You say I'm being turned. Please — please explain it to me. Because I cannot, I do not, for the life of me, understand."

"Please!" I say.

Raul strolls to the armchair and settles down. He gestures for me to come to him. Instead, I sit on the edge of the bed. Raul goes still as a statue and a silence stretches between us. It lasts one minute, two, three.

He's completely unperturbed by it. But I get uncomfortable. I pick at the hem of my dress, suddenly feeling too exposed in the lacy garment.

"That dress, or one very much like it, once belonged to someone special to me," he announces. I stare. "That is why I reacted the way I did when I saw you. That's not to say — I never meant — that you are not beautiful."

He thinks me beautiful?

I blush and shake my head. "Explain the other things. Please."

"Well," he exhales. "Let's start at the top. By now you know where you are. This is The Haven. It is a sort of sanctuary for..." he pauses. "My kind."

"For vampires," I breathe.

"Yes," he says. "For them."

Suddenly, he stands and walks to the balcony. He is more restless than I. "This place was established over six-hundred years ago by the woman you met. She has ruled ever since. I —" he gives a mock bow, "— am one of her three sons."

I nod. More pieces are falling into place.

"The Haven is protected by a powerful series of wards that hide it from those on the Outside. Vampires are the ruling class." He gestures around the room. "We live in modern luxury. The people down there..." his fingers press against the glass, "are trapped in an older age. It's easier, you see," he sneers, "to keep them ignorant of how much the world has changed."

My stomach seizes up in disgust. "That's horrible," I say.

"Yes," Raul agrees. "But necessary. If any of the villagers had an idea of the things humans are capable of now..."

He trails off, shaking his head.

"You keep them as slaves," I mutter. "Blind and deaf to their potential. And you *feed* on them! Don't you? I heard the screams."

"Usually, it's not so violent," he says. He faces me. "You understand why I'm explaining this to you, yes? Because there *is* no going back, Eleira. The things you've seen, all that you know, even if I wanted to let you go, I could not."

My breath catches. "You... want... to let me go?"

"I didn't say that." He grunts. His hands open and close. "You weren't supposed to be thrown into the midst of things the way you were. There was a *process* that was supposed to be followed, and… Argh! It kills me that it wasn't adhered to."

"You planned my abduction." I shiver. "How long have you been watching me?"

He gives a mirthless laugh. "Do you want the truth?"

I nod.

"Since the day you were born."

I gasp.

"Your birth was written in the stars. And I know that is such a cliché, it's so trite and perhaps even expected, but it's the truth."

I swallow the lump in my throat. "What makes me so special?" I wonder.

"Your ancestry does," he tells me. "And you have… The Spark."

"The Spark? The Spark of what?"

"Of magic," he says, completely poker-faced. "You are like Morgan. You possess her powers. And you —"

I can't help it. In light of everything I've seen and been told, I burst out laughing.

"You think — you think I can do *magic?*" The laughter is uncontrollable now, and probably of a hysterical sort. "No, no. No, no no. I don't have a speck of extra ability anywhere inside me." I spread my hands. "What you see is exactly what you get. I am one hundred and one percent human. Always have been. You should check the charts you consulted again, because I'm sure you have the wrong girl."

I stand up and start for the door. "I'll be going now, if that's all right with you —"

"Sit *down*, Eleira."

Raul's voice whips through me in command. My knees fold of their own accord, and I'm right back on the edge of the bed.

Raul comes toward me. "I thought I was doing you a mercy, explaining the how and why of things. But I can see that I made a mistake. I thought that you were mature for your age. But I was wrong there, too. Goodbye, Eleira. I'll see you after you've calmed down."

"No, no, wait, wait, wait!" I grab his hand and pull him back. "I'm listening, please, don't go."

He looks at me in wonder. "I could end your life with one bite," he says. "Does that not scare you?" He glances at our linked hands. "Does who I am not *repulse* you?"

"I... I don't know," I admit. I let his hand go and sag down. "This is all so overwhelming. How can I deny what I see with my own eyes? Then again, everything I see goes against every bit of knowledge I have in my head..." I trail off. "It's just so confusing." I almost cry. "I feel like I've been through the ringer."

Raul's gaze softens. "I understand," he says finally. "But it doesn't mean I can afford to take sympathy on you. I'm sorry. That's the way it has to be."

He turns and walks again to the door.

"Oh. One more thing," he adds before he leaves. "Just in case you're wondering: the sun does not shine here. It's always night. That is one of the protective spells that keeps The Haven safe. I understand it adds to the confusion for a human brought in from the Outside."

And, on that note, I'm alone again.

***

Morgan enters my chambers a few hours later and immediately expresses her delight with what she sees.

"You look wonderful!" she exclaims, gliding to me and beckoning me to rise. "Oh, just look at you! You see, I knew you had enough feminine beauty for it to come out given the right circumstance."

I'm not sure whether that's a compliment or an insult.

I try to give a proper curtsy, of the sort I've only read about but assume she would expect. After all, if she's been Queen for five centuries...

Well, I consider it my best course of action to act meekly around her.

"No, no, none of that," she chastises. "You're doing it all wrong anyway. You put one foot back and bend the knee, like this. Do you see? Oh, don't bother. There's no need for that between us, and besides, you don't have the natural grace to pull it off."

That was *definitely* not a compliment.

"Raul has been by, yes? He's seen you like this?" The Queen smiles. "It must have pleased him to no end to find you so beautiful."

"I wouldn't exactly say that," I mumble.

"Speak up, girl. It won't do for our newest member of royalty to be seen as weak."

I stiffen. "Whatever you're offering, I don't want it. I don't need it. I never asked for it."

Morgan gives me a sympathetic look. "I know, dear. I know. But it is not in our hands to change the tides of fate. You are here now. You are ours. Well —" she laughs, "— you're *mine*. And there's nothing you can do to change that. Oh, you might resist, but I sincerely advise against such stupidity. You've been to The Catacombs. I think you'll consider your lodgings here a vast improvement over that dark and dingy place. And think! All this and more can be yours, if you but lend me a tiny bit of your trust."

How can I trust someone who rules a place like this? I wonder.

Morgan sees the shift on my face. "You're troubled," she notes. "Conflicted, perhaps? Hmm..." she taps her lips. "I have a little surprise for you. I meant to save it for later. Though, perhaps, now you'll take it as a token of goodwill. Hmm?"

She stands up and claps her hands. "You may come in now," she calls.

The doors slowly open. And standing on the threshold, I find a very stoic...

"April," I gasp her name. She looks up and our eyes lock. Hers are storming with all sorts of emotions.

She quickly suppresses those emotions and stands meek as a lamb.

"April here," Morgan says, flowing around her and taking her by her shoulders, "has admitted to being your friend. And I thought, how wonderful! So I cast a little counter-spell..." she snaps her fingers in front of April's nose. The girl flinches. "And ta-dah! Her mind has been restored, and her eyes have been opened to all that she knew before. She came from the Outside, too, you know. But unfortunately, we still can't allow her to think too much of her previous life. It's just safer for all involved. I'm sure you understand."

Morgan smiles. "Well, I'll leave you girls to it. I'm sure you have *plenty* of catching up to do."

April shuffles in. Morgan gives her a dainty kiss on the cheek. Then she closes the doors.

April wastes no time striding right across the floor and swinging her hand at my face in a vicious slap.

"I *hate* you," she announces.

Chapter Twenty-One

RAUL

"I kissed her."

Phillip's head jerks up from the computer screen. "You *what?*"

"I know, I know." I slouch against the wall opposite him. "I couldn't stop myself."

"And she's... still... I mean, is she—"

"She's alive," I grunt. "Unharmed."

"Astounding," Phillip marvels.

"You have *no* idea," I emphasize.

"Before you said I do," he reminds me.

I shake my head. "It's totally different. It's not just hunger. I mean, I've felt hunger before. Real hunger, raw hunger, uncompromising hunger that consumed my whole body and soul."

I snort a laugh. "I'm starting to sound like a poet. But imagine the most terrible hunger you've ever felt, multiply it by ten, and it still wouldn't hold a candle to the *desire* I feel for Eleira."

"Wait." Phillip pushes his glasses up. "*Desire*? Like… between a man and a woman? I thought we were dealing with hunger here?"

"Oh no," I say. "And that's the screwed up thing. I *want* her, Phillip. I want her unlike I've wanted anyone before."

"It's a good thing she's been promised to you —"

I turn around and punch the wall. My fist forms a deep indent. "No!" I snarl. "It's not that simple. She's terrified of me. She puts up a front, but I know. Our kind, what we do, the life we've formed here in The Haven — it disgusts her."

"Just be patient," Phillip advises. "The venom will take her before long. When the transformation begins, all her qualms will disappear. She'll feel the bloodlust, too, and everything will make sense."

"I don't —" I take a deep breath. "I don't think I can do it."

"Do what?"

"Let her transform."

That gets Phillip's full attention. "What? You know the

prophecy. You know what Mother thinks. You —"

"Yes, yes," I interrupt. "But *you* don't know her. She's sweet. She's precious. To take all of that, to take it and strip it away, to destroy all that she is… I can't. I won't be able to live with myself if I do."

"Good thing Mother chose James for the trick," Phillip says.

I slam my fist against the wall again. "You're not listening to me!"

"I am," Phillip promises. "It's not my fault if you're speaking nonsense."

I glare at my brother. He has always been someone I could come to for good advice.

This isn't the sort I thought he'd give.

"Look, Raul," Phillip says. "She's already been infected. Her blood's tainted. Even if you wanted to change it, what could you do? There's no vampire alive who can reverse the poison's spread."

"There must be some way," I say. "You're the scholar, you're the intelligent one! Go to the library, see what you can find. We were *not* the first vampires on earth, no matter what Mother makes the others believe. And we're not the only ones here now. Maybe the other covens know something we don't. Maybe —"

"You're speaking of treason," Phillip murmurs. "You won't go against our coven just for her."

"I'm not going *against* anyone!" I snarl.

"You know communication between covens is forbidden."

"By our own Mother!" I nearly scream. "We've followed her rules for so long —"

"Because she's the Queen," Phillip says.

"So?" I demand. "We both know she wants out. That's why she needs Eleira. Mother is bound to The Haven. She cannot leave, not like us. She's going crazy. She won't say it, but she cannot stand the idea of being here for another five centuries. That's why the succession is so important to her. Eleira will take her place, Eleira will be bound to us, and the same spells that keep Mother here will lock Eleira away from the world for good!"

"Don't tell me your loyalties have been shifted from your own family." Phillip's voice is soft but stern. "We need you, brother. Would you forget who you are and what we've done for the sake of a human girl?"

It's not that simple, I want to say again. Instead, I sigh.

"I don't know," I admit. "I just — do me the favor, won't you? See if you can find anything about reversing the curse. I know it's unlikely, but I have to know."

Phillip looks at me and then nods. "I'll see what I can do."

Chapter Twenty-Two

ELEIRA

"What the hell is wrong with you?" I scream at April.

"Me?" she demands. "Me? It's *you* who's ruined my life!"

We've both gotten our fair share of slaps and hair pulls in, and we've now resorted to having a war of words. Or a screaming war, in any case...

"I saved you from being taken!"

"Yeah, and I saved you from The Convicted! So we were even, and then you had to go and — you had to go and get the Queen involved!"

"Me?" I can't hide the incredulity in my voice. "You think I have any influence over what the *Queen* does?"

She gives me an evil look. "Don't pretend ignorance."

"Um, hello!" I cry out. "I'm a prisoner here, in case you haven't noticed!"

"Oh yeah," April scoffs. She looks around the posh room.

"You've got it *real* bad here."

"You — arr, you're infuriating!" I hurl myself on the bed.

"Look at yourself," April sneers. "You've got the best rooms, the prettiest clothes, and you're complaining? What's wrong with you?"

"What is *wrong* is that I don't want any of this!" I say.

"Well, wake up and smell the roses, Princess, because it's what you've got! And now, thanks to you, I'm completely ostracized. Even worse, I have my memory back!"

"You say that like it's a bad thing." What I wouldn't give to be able to remember the hours — days? — between my stop in the library and waking up in The Haven.

"Of course it's a bad thing! Now I know *where we are.*"

"Like you didn't before?"

She exhales and brushes a loose strand of hair from her face. "Before, I knew where I was, but I didn't know it in relation to what's Outside. I was blissfully ignorant."

"But you came from there!"

"So they locked away those memories of before. And now, thanks to you, they've all come back, and, and..."

She breaks down and falls into a chair. She starts to cry.

"I remember it all, Eleira," she tells me between sobs. "I remember my mother, my father. I remember my younger brother Robin. I remember high school. I remember my friends. I remember my *life!*"

"I thought you'd be thankful if you got that back," I say.

She glared at me through red-rimmed eyes. "You don't understand anything, do you? Those memories do not belong to me anymore. They are not a *part* of me anymore. I can — I can never go back. Obviously not, none of us can, not after we're taken. But the vampires do us a favor by wiping our minds, Eleira. They do it to reduce the pain. *This* is the life we know, the life we have." She stabs a finger into her palm. "Here, at The Haven. Not out there. Not Outside. Here! And I was happy here, before you came along and ruined everything!"

"You were brainwashed," I say. "When you were taken... or rather—what did Raul call it? You were... bewitched."

"Yes! And that gave me peace, don't you see? Peace that I will never have again."

Once more she breaks into sobs.

I hesitate. April is vulnerable. She's vulnerable because of me.

I push myself up. I've never been good at giving comfort. But right now I owe it to April to try.

I come up to her. I bend down and put my hands on her knees. I look into her eyes.

"Listen," I say. "I'm sorry for all of that. It wasn't my intention to get you involved. But since we can't go back in time and change things, we might as well try to make the best of it. Don't you think?"

She eyes me skeptically. She runs her palms over her cheeks to wipe away some of the tears.

"I remember who I was, too." I continue. "And I haven't given up. Not even close. I have every intention of getting out, of escaping —"

"You can't." She gives a sad laugh. "Trust me. I know. That's the first thing that came to mind when the Queen... *restored* me. And you know what she said? Do you want to know what she told me, right after she cast the counter-spell?"

I shake my head. "What?"

"She said I've been marked. She warned that if I try to leave

The Haven, all she'd have to do is give a quick snap of her fingers —" April demonstrates, "— and she'd stop my heart. Just like that."

"No," I breathe.

"Oh yes." April smiles. "So you see? The situation is hopeless. It's not like we can even get past the wards. We—"

"Wait a minute." I stress. "The wards! Didn't Raul say something, back in the Catacombs, about James leaving? And they brought *me* in from out there, just like they did you! If there was a way in for us, there must be a way out…"

She shakes her head. "Only vampires can leave The Haven. Not humans."

"How do you know?" I insist. "Has anyone ever tried? Or are they all just bewitched into believing they can't, just like you were?"

"I —" April frowns. "I'm not sure." Then she gives an exasperated gasp. "But it doesn't matter! You're not hearing me. The Queen will *stop my heart.* I can't go anywhere."

"I heard you," I say. "I just refuse to believe the situation is as hopeless as they want us to think."

April gives me a strange look again. "Hopeless? It's not hopeless for you. You're to become one of *them.*"

And then it hits me. The underlying reason for all of April's resentful behavior.

She's envious.

"I don't want to become one of them," I tell her.

"It doesn't matter," she says.

"It does," I stress. "I'm going to help you. I promise. Whatever way you think I've wronged you, I'll fix it. You're the only friend I have. And I don't want to lose you this soon."

She searches my eyes for a long moment. "You think I'm your... friend?" she asks finally.

"Aren't you?" I ask. "Forget the fight. We're in this together, whatever it is, and I won't abandon you now. We may have had a rocky start, but that doesn't mean we can't fix things in the future."

"I don't believe it," she mutters. "I can't believe you would call me a friend after what I did."

"It's forgiven," I say. "Forgotten. Water under the bridge. All in the past." I hold out my hand. "So what do you say? Can we move on? Because I truly believe that we are weaker apart — and stronger together."

She marvels at me. "You are quite something, you know that?" She giggles and takes my hand. "But okay. I accept. We can be friends."

"Good." I smile. "And the first thing we have to figure out is how to get into the village below."

Chapter Twenty-Three

ELEIRA

After a useless hour trying all the doors and windows in the room, and finding them just as much locked as before, April and I come to the same conclusion: we're trapped.

"So much for that," she huffs. "All we can really do is wait for the next vampire to show up. You think it's going to be Raul?"

"Who knows?" I mutter. I hate the feeling of being cooped up. "Could be the serving girl."

"Who?" she asks.

"You know, the girl who brought me food before." I gesture vaguely to the door. "Quiet. Meek. Didn't want to look up at me."

"Was she human?" April sounds astounded.

"Um, yeah, as far as I could tell."

"I didn't know they let humans up here," April murmurs.

I give a coy smile. "Looks like you don't know everything."

"I never said I did."

"Relax!" I hold my hands up. "I was just kidding."

"Sorry," she shrugs. "It just makes me uneasy, you know? The waiting. *You* know what's going to happen to you. *I* don't."

"Whatever they do with me, you're not leaving my side," I reiterate. "I told Raul I need a guide. Maybe he didn't accept, but the Queen definitely did."

"Hm," she says.

There comes a timid knock at the door. April and I spin to it. The handle turns, and the nameless serving girl opens it.

"I've been asked to bring both of you to the Queen," she says, keeping her eyes on the floor.

I look at April. She nods.

"Let's go."

***

I keep my eyes open and try to take in as much of the surroundings as I can. The penthouses are linked by extravagant bridges sweeping through the trees. Some have soft canopy roofs, while others are exposed to the sky above.

The Haven is spectacular — at least above ground. It's a mix of old and new, of wonderfully crafted carpentry enhanced by modern features like keyless entry systems and motion-detecting doors. Glass and steel blend seamlessly with beautiful, golden wood.

"Wow," April whispers behind me. "I had no idea that the vampires had... all this."

I don't disagree. The wealth and splendor of this part of The Haven is unrivaled.

My gaze goes down past a railing. The wealth up here is unrivaled, but it only emphasizes the stark poverty below us.

None of that sits well with me.

"Come on," the serving girl says. "You don't want to keep the Queen waiting."

"No," I mutter underneath my breath. "We definitely don't."

Another few minutes and we reach a swirling staircase running around the trunk of a tree. We go down. When we reach the bottom and step out onto the path, April's eyes widen.

"I've been here," she manages. "Right here, I've passed this spot so many times. But I never—" she looks at the staircase and shudders. "I never had any clue *that* existed."

There are people walking in groups of twos and threes around us. They keep their voices hushed. I catch the eyes of one boy, who's gaping openly at us.

He jumps and runs off.

"I think he thinks we appeared out of thin air," April tells me. "That's what it would have looked like to him."

I nod, taking it all in. The *injustice* of this way of life is gnawing at me.

The girl leading us continues down a path through the trees, and we follow.

I notice something strange about her. Her eyes never leave the ground, except when she's speaking to us. It's like she's being led by a string.

I mention it to April, who murmurs her agreement thoughtfully. "It's probably a variation of the same bewitchment cast on me," she says. "It allows her to go *up* without really seeing anything."

A breeze ruffles my dress, and I shiver. Not from the cold.

We walk through a densely wooded area. Starlight from above provides just enough light to navigate, but not much more.

Suddenly, the trees open, and we're in a vast clearing. Standing in the midst of it is an enormous Gothic castle complete with angled spires and curving towers and jagged parapets. It's beautiful and astounding and *old*, and it's nothing I would have expected, but I've seen enough not to be surprised.

The girl walks us to the entrance. "This is as far as I'm to take you," she says. "You'll wait inside for the Queen."

I look around the grand lobby. There are chandeliers hanging from the ceiling. Every single candle is lit. There are paintings on the walls, depicting men and women in ornate dress. The strangest thing about them is that every time my eyes move past them, the portraits seem to *shift*. Yet as soon as I direct my eyes back, they are completely still, exactly as a painting should be.

"Okaaay," I say, more than a tad uncomfortable. "This is *not* creepy at all."

Laughter greets my proclamation. I look up and find Morgan descending the grand staircase. She's changed into a flowing white dress with a transparent shawl draped around her shoulders. She looks beautiful as always.

"Do you like them?" she asks. She walks to the nearest painting and runs her hand along the gilded frame. "I can tell you who they were, if you'd like to know. Each one of them," she smiles at me, "is trapped here for a reason."

I give a start. "Excuse me?"

"Oh yes," Morgan continues. "Each one of these vampires thought him or herself capable of bettering me." She flutters to the next portrait over. It's of a striking woman with long, sleek black hair.

"This, for example, was my dear cousin Rebecca." Morgan turns and puts on the same expression as Rebecca has in the painting. "You see the resemblance, don't you?"

It's not immediate, but I nod... slowly.

"Rebecca was one of the first to take issue with my rule. I endured her criticism for as long as I could. After all, we *were* family. But then, one day, oh!" Morgan gasps, and brings her hands over her chest. "A little bird brought me word of a plot to assassinate me in my sleep. The person behind it?" She taps the painting. "None other than my own cousin."

Morgan walks toward me. "I do have a weakness, you know,"

she says. "And that is my soft heart. While Rebecca may have been cruel and evil, and intent on ending my life with no remorse, I could never bring myself to do the same thing. Snuffing out a vampire's life is one of the greatest crimes imaginable. After all, each of us has been imbued with immunity from disease, from age, from sickness. We are the angels of the earth. To kill one of us…" Morgan shakes her head sadly. "It is a ruination of the world's most precious beauty."

I find myself backing up slowly as she speaks.

"But I could not simply leave her unpunished, now, could I? Then I would be seen as weak. Maybe others would get the same idea. Maybe others would stage," she glances at April, "an uprising."

Abruptly she slips behind April and grabs her hair. My friend yelps in surprise. Morgan cruelly twists April's head to one side, exposing the expanse of her neck.

"An uprising," the Queen purrs in her ear, "of the sort your kind is whispering about right now."

And suddenly, Morgan sinks her fangs into April's neck.

I cry out. April goes limp. She doesn't fight. As soon as Morgan's lips are on her, it's like all control has evaporated from her body.

It's over before I can do anything to help. Morgan pulls up and wipes her mouth with the back of one hand. Two tiny red dots are visible on April's neck, but aside from that, I see no blood.

"The 'Little Drink,'" Morgan explains to me. She lets April go. The girl blinks, dazed, and takes a step forward. Her eyes are glazed over.

"What..." she begins.

Morgan comes around her front and takes her by the shoulders. "Oh my," she murmurs. "You're a little woozy there, aren't you?"

April nods, without any sort of recognition. "Yes," she says. "But who are you —"

Then she gasps, and her eyes go wide in terror. "My Queen!"

"Oh, pah-pah," Morgan says gently. "Don't you worry about that." She holds a hand to April's forehead. "How are you feeling, dear?"

April's eyes flash to me. "Fine," she says, hesitantly. "Why — why am I here? Did you... did you call me?"

"Oh yes," Morgan says. "Otherwise, why would you be in the presence of your Queen?" She leans in and gives the girl a quick kiss on the cheek. "Run away, now, right back to Eleira. I'm not sure how the two of you got separated with me in between."

April does exactly as she's told. As she comes toward me, Morgan tilts her head to the side, smiles, and mouths behind her back, *"She doesn't remember."*

My eyes widen in understanding.

"What was I saying?" the Queen asks. "Oh, right. We were discussing my cousin's treachery. Well, I didn't want to kill her, of course not, but I couldn't let her crime go unpunished. So I came up with the most beautifully *intricate* solution!"

She comes back to the portrait.

"I severed her soul from her body and bound it within the canvas. Just like I would do to any," her eyes flash at me, full of meaning, "who would think to try the same against me now."

Chapter Twenty-Four

RAUL

I race through the village, heart pounding. I grab the nearest human.

"Eleira!" I exclaim. "Have you seen Eleira?"

The woman shies back, terrified. "N-no."

I let her go, forgotten, and go to the next one. A man, in his early forties. "Have you seen a girl," I demand, "this high, dark hair, wearing a dress?"

He shakes his head quickly. "Not here, master."

I curse. When I came to Eleira's chambers, and found them empty, alarm took me. None but I have the authority to release her. I'm terrified that one of the other vampires caught scent of her blood and found it impossible to resist, even if they knew that she was *mine*…

"I'll destroy anyone who lays hands on her," I promise.

I run forward blindly, calling her name, probably looking like a lunatic. The humans know the law. They know they're safe from my kind now—but that doesn't stop them from being frightened by seeing me raging through their midst.

So be it. The only thing on my mind now is finding the girl who's exerted such an insane pull on me.

I turn a corner and come face-to-face with a young serving girl I recognize from my mother's clique. She gasps when she sees me and tries to step aside, but I grasp her by the arms.

"Eleira," I say. "You know her?"

She bobs her head up and down. "Of course, my Prince."

Hope blossoms inside me. "You've *seen* her? Recently?"

"Y–yes." She points the way she came. "I just brought her and her friend to the Queen."

"You *what?*" I yell.

She cringes in fright. I realize I'm hurting her — scaring her with my reaction.

I force my fingers to uncurl from her arms. I level my voice. "You did this by the Queen's command?"

"Of course," she breathes.

I sigh in relief. "Thank you," I say. "For being honest with me."

She gives me a look of complete surprise. For a second, I wonder why, and then I realize. If she's mostly dealt with my mother and my older brother James — they share the same faction of servants — then she would never have expected words of gratitude to come from the lips of a vampire.

I step around her. She's already forgotten as I start to race toward my mother's castle.

But then she calls out, "If the girl is important to you —"

I stop and turn around. I'm on her in an instant. "Yes?" I press.

The serving girl takes a deep breath. The next words seem to take all of her resolve. "If she's important to you, then I wouldn't interrupt. The Queen, I heard her say, she cast a spell on her."

"What?" That's news to me. "What kind of spell?"

"I don't know," she dry washes her hands nervously. "I just heard her say... accidentally, you see, I wasn't eavesdropping..."

"Yes, yes, get on with it," I growl, losing patience.

"I heard her say that Eleira's days are running out, *unless* she follows the Queen's exact orders."

I grunt. That could be in reference to a million different things.

The girl drops her gaze. "I'm sorry, I shouldn't have said anything. It's probably nothing, but I just thought... well, never mind."

She gives a little curtsy and turns to go.

"Hold on." I catch her arm. Fear flashes in her eyes. I'm still scowling, so I force myself to smile in a somewhat reassuring way.

At least I *hope* it's reassuring.

"You did well," I tell her. "What's your name?"

"Monica, my Lord," she whispers.

I doubt any vampire has ever asked her name before.

I soften my voice. "You don't need to be frightened of me, Monica. I appreciate your help. I'm not like my brother. If he - if he harasses you, on his return, you can come to me. I will make him stop."

"That's very gracious of you," she stammers, "But the Prince has never done anything bad —"

She gasps and cuts off when I lift her hand and expose her

wrist to reveal the bite marks hidden there. "Only *James* leaves marks like these," I tell her softly.

She jerks her hand away and looks extraordinarily ashamed.

"I won't press," I promise. "But if you ever need help you can come to me."

"Thank you," she whispers.

I nod and let go, then run the rest of the way to the castle.

Chapter Twenty-Five

ELEIRA

The Queen takes us on an elaborate tour of the castle, chatting frivolously the whole way through. Her easy manner is completely at odds with the horrors she show us.

The portraits were just the start. The men and women — vampires — inside there *do* move, but only when they are unwatched. They're like prisoners struggling in straitjackets. Their bodies are locked more or less in place. But they still fight to break free of the restraints.

The rest of the castle is no better. There are rooms we go through that I'm sure are dedicated only to torture. They are side-by-side with those adorned with fancy throws and beautiful beds and all sorts of comforts, the rooms dedicated to pleasure.

I hear and sense the presence of others in here with us, but I never see them. I don't know if they're vampires or humans. I don't even know if it matters much at this point.

Eventually we reach the throne room. It's a huge, open

space, empty except for a single gold chair raised high on a dais. Its back is inlaid with shining crystals that rise halfway to the ceiling, like an enormous growth of rock. The higher they go, the more jagged their edges get.

I swallow on my first look at it. It's very intimidating.

Morgan walks straight to it, her dress flowing behind her, and flutters down. "Oh!" she says when she sees me standing. "Come, come. Take your proper place."

She snaps her fingers, and in a puff of dark smoke, a hard iron stool appears beside the throne. Right when it happens, my vision goes red, and a sharp pain stabs through my temple.

"Ah!" I cry out.

April looks at me in concern but says nothing. She's more intimidated by the Queen than I am.

The pain fades a second later. I blink in confusion. *What was that?*

"Well?" the Queen beckons. "What's taking you so long? You don't want to keep your monarch waiting..." She raps her nails against the armrest.

I share a look with April and slowly climb the steps. As I

climb higher and higher, an uncanny feeling of being watched creeps over me. The Queen's eyes are directed outward. She has a coy smile on her face.

I approach the stool apprehensively. There are small metal barbs on the back half. It's really something you're only meant to perch on.

Just another way to make me uneasy.

I smooth the back of my dress, turn around to sit—and freeze with a sudden gasp.

The entire auditorium, which had been empty only a moment ago, is now teeming with vampires.

I know what they are because of how absolutely still they stand. Not a single one of them stirs. They're like wax statues. All their eyes are on me. They line the sides of the chamber, dressed in rich fabrics and luxurious outfits that range in style from centuries ago all the way up to modern day.

And they're all, each one, stunningly beautiful. Their figures are somehow enhanced compared to ordinary humans. The males have more power in their stance. The women have curves that are subtly more emphatic than usual. All the faces are striking, bold, aristocratic.

April is the only one who stands out in the mass. She's completely stiff and unmoving, but in a different way. Her eyes wander side-to-side, betraying her fear. Her poor peasant girl's clothes don't help the contrast.

"How did they..." I begin.

Morgan looks at me and smiles. "They're waiting for you to sit, Princess."

In a daze, I lower myself onto the stool. As soon as I do, movement breaks out in the crowd. The vampires start talking, whispering to each other, just as I would expect in a regular assembly of so many people.

So many 'people?' Is that the right phrase?

But I don't know what else I would call them. After all, they do look like *people,* enhanced, uplifted, extraordinarily beautiful people.

Goosebumps wash over me.

Morgan raises a hand. A silence immediately falls. Now the attention shifts away from me and to her.

"You all know why you've been summoned," she announces. "But your future sovereign here does not. This is Eleira," she swirls a hand over me, "and though some of you may have heard of her arrival, it is the first time you can see her yourselves, see that she is real, and that—yes—-she is still human."

Hostile murmurs come from the mass. I grip the bottom of my seat so tightly my nails feel like they're about to rip off.

"Oh!" Morgan says suddenly. "I almost forgot. We are also *blessed* by the presence of one other human." Her eyes fall on April. "Come up here, dear, won't you?"

I get a very, very bad feeling about this.

April reluctantly climbs the steps. Morgan holds out her hand. April goes to one knee and kisses the ring on the Queen's finger.

"Good girl," Morgan murmurs. "You know the proper protocols." She draws her hand away and gestures dismissively to my side. "Now, take your place behind Eleira."

April walks to me and steps one foot back. I start to turn my head to her, but she quickly hisses, "No!"

I snap my attention forward.

"As you can see," Morgan continues. "The two girls have developed a particular bond. Neither of them is to be touched by *any* vampire. You will spread the message amongst your peers who could not make it today. If any harm befalls Eleira or her hand-servant, well..." Morgan's lips curl up in a cruel smile, "...whoever is responsible will have to answer to me. Is that understood?"

The absolute silence that follows the warning is more ominous than any other reaction I could have envisioned.

"Now then!" Morgan claps her hands. "We've got that out of the way, it's time to turn our attention to the real matter that brought you here."

On her words, the far entrance doors heave open. Two vampires, both in chains, are dragged forth by a circle of guards.

The murmurs pick up as the two prisoners come to a stop before us. The guards kick them to the floor.

Both look... awful. Their skin is stretched so tight over their bones they might as well be skeletons. Their eyes are sunken and red. There's not a trace of hair on either of them—it's almost like it has all been burned away.

I suck in a breath when I realize one of them is a woman. She's so thin and wretched... only the contours of her eyes hint at her femininity.

"You know the charges laid against you," Morgan says, almost casually. "How do you plead?"

"Innocent!" they call out in unison.

Morgan looks at them and laughs. The assembled vampires take cue from her reaction. They start to laugh, cruelly, as well.

The prisoners huddle down, defeated.

Morgan calls for silence. "My son James saw both of you consorting with a band of humans the night before The Hunt. Do you deny the accusation?"

"Yes!" The male vampire looks up. He holds his hands out pleadingly. "Patricia and I would never go against you. We owe you everything! Our lives, our powers. Please!"

Morgan arches an eyebrow. "You would call my son a liar?"

"No!" The man shakes his head. "No. Never. But the situation was not as it appeared. It —"

"Enough." Morgan cuts him off. "I won't tolerate babbling. You, Jacob, are also accused of lying with a human. How do you plead?"

Behind me, April makes an almost imperceptible gasp and takes one tiny step back. "Jacob," she whispers.

"That…" Jacob spreads his hands, "That…"

Then his eyes fall on April, and he lets out a roar. "It's her!" he screams. "She was the one I found with your son, *she* was the one who framed me, she —"

He cuts off when one of the guards places a boot in his back. "You will show proper respect to your Queen, worm," the guard growls.

But Morgan seems amused by the new information. "Could it be…?" she murmurs. She beckons April closer. "Come here, dearest. Let me take a good look at you."

April shakes her head. "No," she whimpers, oh so softly. "It wasn't me. I didn't."

"*Now*," the Queen snaps.

Shaking, trembling, April approaches her monarch.

"You don't need to be frightened," Morgan assures her softly. "I just want to take a look at you." She holds her hand out, palm up. "Let me see your wrist."

April swallows and extends her arm. The Queen catches it. Their eyes meet. The whole assembly is watching.

Morgan pulls April's sleeve back. The girl flinches. I see two fresh bite marks on her arm. And then, the most astounding thing happens;

Morgan runs her hand over April's wrist, and the marks disappear.

The Queen surges up and holds April's arm out. "There is nothing!" she announces. "You, Jacob, are a criminal and a liar."

"No, no, no," he says. "It was her, it was the girl —"

The guard kicks him again. "Silence, cur."

I look around the room, questions boiling in my mind. The Queen just protected April. *Why?*

"It falls on me to pass sentence," Morgan says. "I find both of the accused guilty, for the crimes described —"

The two entrance doors crash open, cutting her off mid-sentence. Everyone's head swings back.

There, standing in the middle of the threshold, is Raul. He looks furious.

"Oh," Morgan's eyebrows go up. "How kind of you to join us."

"I would have been here earlier, *Mother*," he says. "If I had known you'd advanced the trial by six hours."

She feigns surprise. "You weren't informed?"

Raul walks forward. He glances at me once. That's all the acknowledgement I get.

"It's fortunate I make a habit of keeping an eye on things," he says. "When so many of our kind go missing from their regular places of activity, it's obvious they've been summoned."

"I assure you it was not my intention to do this without you," Morgan says sweetly. "I just wanted to show Eleira how we deliver justice in The Haven."

"Justice?" Raul laughs. He stops by the two prisoners. They flinch away, but he bends down and whispers something first in Patricia's ear, then in Jacob's. Cautiously relieved expressions blossom on their faces.

Raul looks up and addresses his mother. "You call this sham of a trial *justice?*"

"Their guilt is doubtless," Morgan says smoothly. "All evidence points to their fault in the crimes described."

"And where is the *accuser?*" Raul says. "Where is James, the one who brought about the charge?"

Morgan hisses. "Everybody knows your brother is on an important diplomatic mission —"

"And so the trial will be delayed until he returns, or you will simply throw out these ludicrous charges." Raul stares right into the Queen's eyes and speaks with authority I did not know he had. "Our citizens deserve fairness, and all the rights afforded to them as subjects of The Haven. I will *not* let you condemn these two without due process."

Morgan surges up. "You *dare* go against me?" she screams. "You dare –"

"No," Raul says. "All I dare is remind you of the laws governing our home and make sure that those laws are upheld equally for all."

I don't know why, but I feel a sudden sense of admiration for Raul.

"Gah!" Morgan hisses. She's in a rage. "Out, out, get out, all of you!"

The assembly of vampires stream out the door. In mere seconds we're left with only Raul, the guards, and Jacob and Patricia for company.

Morgan paces back and forth in front of her throne. Her brows are furrowed in anger. She looks extremely bitter.

"That," she tells her son, "was a grave miscalculation."

"No, Mother," he replies. "The mistake was yours. If our coven saw justice distributed unfairly —"

"Our coven *knows* that my word is law!" she screams.

Raul's eyes flash to me. "Not for much longer," he murmurs.

I swallow.

They stare at each other for a tense moment. April cowers beyond sight. Patricia and Jacob remain still on the floor.

I can't take it anymore. I break the silence.

"What's going to happen to them?" I blurt out, looking at the two chained vampires.

The Queen turns to me and acknowledges my comment. "Yes, Raul," she says. "What *is* going to happen to them?"

"They will return to custody until James comes back —"

"Impossible," his mother breaks in. "I will not have them brought back into the village where they can go stir more trouble. Unless..." she taps her lips, and her eyes focus on me. "Eleira can have them."

"What!" I gasp, at the same time as Raul says, "No!"

"Why not?" Morgan sneers. "She will have to get used to being in the presence of our kind. If you are so sure of their innocence, why, you should have no problem leaving them near Eleira. Unless... you foresee other problems?"

Raul looks at the two vampires on the ground. They're still kneeling, unsure and hesitant. The guards make an impenetrable ring around them.

Finally, he says, "*I* will stand for them."

"Don't be a fool!" Morgan erupts. "They are of the lowest caste. Look how they tremble in your shadow!"

"No, Mother," he says softly. "It is you they are fearful of. You do not have their respect. You have their hatred."

She laughs. "What do I care if criminals detest me? I see no other way. I am the one who *executes* their sentence."

All of this bickering is going over my head. The last thing I want is to get entrenched in petty politics, especially as nothing more than a bystander. I need to retreat from this situation, to go back somewhere, to have time to *think*.

"If you want a true succession," Raul tells the Queen, "and if you want it done without rebellion, you will take to heart what your subjects think. Leave Jacob and Patricia with me, and I will ensure they do not trouble you."

Morgan casts him a filthy look. "Fine!" she says finally. "But I hope you know what you are doing."

And with that, she flies down the steps from the throne, beckons the guards to follow her, and leaves me and April alone with Raul and the two prisoners.

Chapter Twenty-Six

RAUL

I see her sitting there beside my Mother's throne, and all I can think is how beautiful she is.

It's wreaking havoc with my brain. It's not enough that her blood smells the way it does. No, she has to be stunningly beautiful, too.

And the way she's regarding me now, with a mix of fear and wonder — I hate it. I wish I could tell her the things she does to me. But I barely understand them myself.

Besides, it's not as if she'll simply open up herself to me.

So I shift focus to the two prisoners still kneeling on the floor. "You need to feed," I tell them.

"Yes!" Patricia gasps. "Yes, we've been deprived for so long…"

Deprived and left in the sun, I think. That's the only explanation for their current condition. Vampires can last weeks, maybe months, without a drop of blood. The cravings will take them, but they would not appear as these two do before me.

My Mother's methods of torture disgust me.

"You know where the blood banks are," I say. "I will grant you some of the supply from them."

"Oh, thank you!" Patricia exclaims.

I grimace. "Don't grovel."

She pulls back. "I'm sorry, I meant no disrespect —"

"Save it," I say. My main concern is separating Patricia and her husband from Eleira and April. They're in chains now, but if the bloodlust takes them and they try to go for the two girls — I will have no choice but to destroy them.

After the whole scene I caused in my Mother's court, I'm reticent to be responsible for that.

"Come," I say. The two of them stand. It's pitiful, the state they're in, but nothing can be done for it now.

Eleira stands as we're leaving. "Are you just going to leave us here?"

"I'll be back," I promise, not looking over my shoulder. "As soon as I deal with these two."

Once outside of Mother's castle, I grab both Jacob's and Patricia's chain. "How fast can you move?" I ask them.

They look at each other. "Not very."

"Then I'm sorry for this," I say, "but we have to be quick."

I start off with immense speed, dragging both of them behind me in the dirt.

We reach my residence. They're dirty and soiled and look worse than before.

But they don't complain about my method of transport.

I let them in. "I'll get somebody to bring you the blood I promised," I say. "For now, stay inside, stay quiet, and do *not* be seen. There are those who would try to curry favor with my mother by going against me and ending your lives. Do you understand?"

The two weakened vampires nod and mutter their gratitude.

"Don't thank me yet," I say. "We're nowhere near to being out of the woods."

In fact, we've only just wandered in.

***

The trek back to the castle takes longer than I would like. Vampires from the assembly try to speak to me about what transpired. I entertain the briefest of conversations, the whole time thinking only of the two girls I left in the throne room.

When I return, I'm relieved to find Eleira and April both still there.

They go still when they see me. Suspicion blooms in their eyes. I walk toward April first. "Go," I tell her softly, "I need to speak to Eleira alone."

Eleira takes April's hand. "Whatever you want to tell me, she can hear," she says. "The Queen restored her memory. She knows who and where she is."

I frown. "Is that so?" I had no idea Mother would risk so much. For what? To make Eleira feel comfortable?

April nods, defiant toward me. "She and I are in this together."

"You realize your little friendship will not last?" I demand of them. "Eleira, you're set to become like me. April, you're destined to remain human."

"She knows," Eleira says. "Why would that change anything?"

I scoff. "Do you really believe becoming a *vampire* won't change you?" I step toward April. "I can resist her. But I've had centuries of experience. You think *you* won't want to drain her of every last drop of her red, sweet, precious, life-giving *human* blood the moment the transformation hits?"

Even speaking of feeding threatens my resolve not to touch April.

I quickly change the subject and lower my voice. "But... there might be a way to delay it."

"What?" Eleira asks. At the same time, April exclaims, "Why!"

"To give Eleira more time," I say, focusing on the girl I feel so protective of. "You've been thrown into this headfirst. You're not getting out. There is no escape from The Haven for you. But that does not mean I'm not willing to help you come to grips with who you are."

"I know who I am," she says haughtily. The spark is back in her eyes.

"Yes," I say. "But you don't know all that we expect from you."

"You expect me to be someone I'm not," she tells me, straight-up. "Someone I never was."

"But someone you were born to be," I say. My gaze goes around the empty chamber. "Don't let Mother hear that doubt. We are in her domain. The walls have ears. You never know who might be listening."

Eleira takes a small step back. I can see her fright and the desperate way she's trying to hide it.

I have the insatiable urge to take her into my arms and give her comfort. But what would she do if I tried? She'd be repelled by me. How can I show her that, in spite of who I am, I *am* on her side in all this?

At least, as much as I can hope to be.

"We need to get out of the castle," I take another look around. "I'll bring you back to your chambers. You're safest there."

I turn away and start to walk out but get the feeling they are not following. I look back. "Well?"

"I don't want to be locked up again," Eleira says resolutely. "I want to see all parts of The Haven. I want to go into the village and meet the people."

I laugh. "I'm afraid that is an impossible request."

"Why?" she demands. "April's been there. She can show me. She can introduce me to the people she knows."

I shake my head. "You don't understand. Vampires and humans keep separate. They do not mingle. We live here together, yes, but the only way the arrangement works is if we both keep to our own parts. Besides," I look her up and down, "world will have spread about you. Nobody would dare speak to you for fear of inciting a vampire's wrath."

April takes a sudden step forward. "*I* speak to her," she says.

"Yes, but you're *different* from the rest of them," I nearly snarl. "You are not so cowering. You have ambitions the other humans would not dream of entertaining. Is it not true *you* lay with my brother? Is it not true *you* are the one who helped frame Jacob and Patricia?"

April wavers under my questions.

"Ha!" I bark. "Just as I thought." I see the surprise on Eleira's face. "Oh, and your friend thought it was a lie, did she?" I ask. I can't help the tempestuous words spilling from my mouth. "She thought the accusations were false? Or maybe your friendship isn't yet on the level I'd assumed. Hmm?"

Both girls stare at me as if I'd transformed into some horrible monster.

"I saw..." Eleira says. "I saw the Queen do something to your arm." She looks at April. "She protected you. Didn't she?"

April nods, but then shakes her head as she says, "I don't know why she did it."

"So you see?" I demand. Both their attention snaps back to me. "You girls are out of your depth. I'm the only one who can offer sanctuary. Will you come with me, or not?" I give a cruel smile. "I'd much rather not have to force you to my will."

Chapter Twenty-Seven

ELEIRA

Raul takes us back to the luxurious chamber in the treetops. This time, however, he offers me a key card.

"It'll work on only the doors you're allowed through," he explains. "Wherever it doesn't open, you shouldn't be."

When I take it from him, our fingers brush. An electric jolt races up my arm.

I suck in a breath and pull away.

Raul's eyes widen, and I know he felt the jolt too.

"Incredible," he murmurs, so softly I almost think I imagine the word.

"What *is* it with you two?" April asks when we're alone. "The way he looks at you…"

I stare at her. "What?"

"Nothing, nothing," she says, holding her hands up. "I didn't mean to sound hostile."

"I'm sorry," I shake my head. "I'm just tired, and over-whelmed, you know? Twenty four hours ago I thought I'd be a Convicted's meal. And now, I've been introduced to all of them here as their *Princess*? It's ludicrous.

April comes up to me and takes my hand. "But you're not in it alone anymore," she promises. "Remember that."

I nod. "Thank you." A yawn comes unbidden. "How long have we been up? It's so strange keeping time when it's always night out."

"It's like we're behind an eclipse," April agrees.

"How do the other humans do it?" I ask as I walk to the bal-cony and look at their primitive village below. "How can they live with no sun?"

"They don't know any other life exists," April says.

"It's so sad," I say. "Those brought in from the Outside get bewitched. Those born here aren't aware of any other way of life." I feel a resolve building inside.

"This is bigger than just me," I mutter. "I'm not the only one being held prisoner. All of these people are, too."

I turn to face April. My resolve is transforming into a new

idea. Into a purpose. "If they want to elevate me to a position of power," I say, "then I'm not going to forget the injustice being done. I *will* free these people, April. I'll free them of this tyranny. Because all of them—every single one—deserve to have their lives back."

Chapter Twenty-Eight

PHILLIP

"...deserve to have their lives back."

I stop the video there and look at Raul. "That's quite the riveting speech she gave."

My brother grunts. "You know, I almost wish she had it in her to do it... or at least to try."

"You don't think she would?"

He smiles sadly. "Not after the transformation takes hold. She'll be like the rest of us. Some might try to do good, but it goes against our nature. We are creatures of the night. And the night is dark and full of terrors."

I laugh a little. "You've been watching that TV show again, haven't you? What's it called? Game of...?"

"Game of Thrones," he says. "And maybe. It's a guilty pleasure."

"What Mother would say if she knew..."

"Mother has her own problems to worry about. Anyway, that's not why I came. Have you made any progress with your search?"

"You mean *your* search," I correct. I sigh. "And no. There's no such thing as an antidote to vampirism. It can't be reversed."

"You need to look harder, Phillip," Raul says. "I *know* there's something there. There has to be. I can feel it!"

"For all your protestations, you're a lot like James, you know that?" I rib him gently. "All passion and energy, just less of the anger."

"Oh no," he said. "There's anger here." He touches his chest. "Lots and lots of anger. Believe me."

I turn back to the computer. "There's no antidote," I repeat. "But I did find *this*," I pull up a scanned image of an ancient parchment.

Raul's attention instantly goes to the screen. "What is it? How'd you get it? Those letters..." his fingers run along the screen. "It's Arabic, isn't it?"

"It's the same alphabet, but not the same language," I say.

"Well, you're the master of tongues! What does it say?"

I grimace in annoyance. "Unfortunately, I can't read it. Not properly. Bits and pieces of it make a little sense—"

"Get on with it," Raul growls. His hands tighten on the back of my chair.

"As best as I can tell," I begin. "It speaks of a ritual. Conducted by the ancient pharaohs of Egypt. They believed," I clear my throat, "they believed some of our abilities came from the Sun God. But that when they tried to transfer the Sun God's abilities onto humans, an evil spirit interrupted the procedure and infused those powers with night." I shake my head. "Like I said, I can't make much sense of it. But it's definitely speaking of what we are."

"This is our origin?" Raul marvels.

"It could be." I admit. "And just as easily, it could not. But the reason I'm showing this to you is that I think — I *think!* — that the ritual they're describing is an attempt at exorcising the bad spirits from the human form and restoring the Sun God's gift to what it was meant to be before it became tainted."

"But then that's it!" Raul exclaims. "That is the solution. That is the cure!

"No," I say. "You're jumping to conclusions. For one, more

than half of the description of the ritual is missing." I scroll through the image of the parchment to show him. "See? Significant parts are lost."

"Why, that's not —" Raul grunts. "That doesn't mean the original is gone. It's just the scan that's missing, isn't it?"

"I wouldn't be so sure."

"Where did you get it, anyway? You never answered my question."

"I... hacked into Father's coven's computers," I admit.

"What!" Raul exclaims. "If it's traced back to us—"

"Don't worry, I have more tact than that. Unlike James's diplomatic mission," I add.

"Okay, good," Raul says. "Have you heard anything from our eldest brother yet?"

"It's only been a few days. No."

Raul makes a sound deep in his throat. "Just keep looking. And for now? Turn the camera off to Eleira's room. I want to give her the privacy she's due."

Chapter Twenty-Nine

ELEIRA

The next few days pass uneventfully. I expect somebody to come for me and April, to get some sort of summons, to be told what to do...

Nothing. We have food brought to us, but there isn't any interaction past that.

That first night back I ventured out with the key card to see what access it grants me. Precious little. All the doors in the hall outside my room remain locked, except for one that leads to a wide balcony facing the opposite way from mine. The view from it is all trees and darkness; the village lies on the other side.

I start to worry about what my family and friends out in the real world think of what happened to me. There's probably a police search going on at this very moment.

I sigh. I've seen enough to know nobody will ever find me.

But eventually... I *will* make my way back. I won't just abandon all that I've known and grown up with. Not for some creatures who shouldn't even exist. Not for the way they pulled me into their twisted games.

"Enjoying the night, Princess?"

I spin around. I hadn't heard anybody enter!

Standing there is a lanky, boyish looking vampire. He has the tell-tale pale skin and enhanced good looks, but something about him feels... different.

He's wearing glasses, for one. I thought all vampires gained perfect vision. And there's something about his hair, too. It's not as sleek, not as shining and healthy and vibrant as every other vampire I'd seen.

"Who are you?" I ask, wary. I back away. "If you know I'm the Princess, you know the Queen's orders. I'm not to be harmed."

His eyebrows go up, and he gives a little laugh. "Harm you? Why ever would I harm you? As appealing as your kind is to some of my kin, I choose not to partake... in their viciousness."

I narrow my eyes. "What do you mean?"

He spreads his hands. "I don't drink human blood."

"What? How is that even possible?" I eye him up and down. "I don't believe you."

"Believe it," he says. He steps to the railing and looks out into the forest. "It's not been easy, mind you. But the thirst... lessens, after so many years."

"So you don't feed at all?" I ask. Something about his honesty intrigues me.

"Oh I feed. But just on animal blood. It's a sacrifice I've consciously made. While other vampires grow stronger every time they take a life and get a new infusion of blood, I simply... linger." He turns his head to me. "Something you could do, if you so choose, when your transformation is complete."

"What's your name?" I ask. "There's something familiar about you, I think."

"That's because you've met both my brothers," he says. "Raul and James."

"You're Phillip!" I exclaim.

He smiles. "The one and only."

"I heard Raul calling for you the first night I was here."

"Ah. About that. I'm sorry, but it was all James's idea. He has a mind for theatrics. He thought it would be," his lips twist in distaste, "*fun* to see how you react waking up in the atrium." He shrugs. "He always liked to play with his food."

I shiver.

Phillip notices. "James won't hurt you," he says. "He's been sent away."

"I know."

"In fact, nobody in The Haven will dare hurt you. They know you have my Mother's protection. And yet..."

Phillip turns to face me. He looks into my eyes.

"I came to warn you, Princess. Not everything here is as it seems. Everything we do gives the appearance of relative peace and prosperity under the Queen's rule, but there are rumblings underground. Not all are happy that you've been chosen as her successor. There are many who would have preferred the true heir came from within our own ranks. That's part of the reason we're turning you, you see. So they won't see you as an upstart, defenseless human—no matter how reluctant you may be. Your enemies will choose not to see that. The truth is... the truth is Mother doesn't need a vampire to rule. She needs a *witch*. That is what you are, through your ancestry. It is one thing you can never deny."

He turns to leave. "Forgive me for interrupting. I wish you a pleasant night."

"Wait!" I say. "Wait, you say you came here with a warning? What is it?"

"Only that you should treasure these peaceful times," he says. "Because they will not last for much longer."

"Wait, no, Phillip, don't go." He's the first vampire I don't feel frightened of. "Nobody is telling me anything. I *heard* about the transformation, but past that, I don't know a thing! Am I supposed to feel different? Because I don't. Is something supposed to happen to my body? Because it hasn't. Maybe it's all just a sham, a way for you to try to endear me to your cause, or, or..." I blubber on. "I don't know."

A look of genuine concern flashes across Phillip's face. "You haven't been told anything about it?" he asks.

I shake my head. "No."

"Well, that's not good..." he taps his lips. "What can I say? You've been injected with James's venom. There's only a tiny bit of it in your blood. There are changes happening within your body right now. They have been since that first night. But they are happening very, very slowly, because you've been given such a miniscule amount.

"The slower it happens, the less risk there is. Mother thought you precious, and so she only let James give you the minimal effective dose. I wouldn't have thought he'd be able to hold back, but my brother might be more disciplined than I've given him credit for."

Phillip steps toward me. "Let me see your eyes," he says. He hesitates, then reaches out and takes hold of my face. His touch does nothing to me. It's completely inert, like a doctor's examination.

"Hmm," he says. "Look this way." He points. "Then that." He points again. Then he lets go.

"Your eyes *are* changing," he says. "It's the most subtle shift. But the eyes are where the transformation first takes hold. And then, the body, and then, the mind..." He trails off and shudders in discomfort.

"What?" I ask. "Is it that unpleasant?"

"You could say that," he sighs. "But I don't want to frighten you."

"How long..." I swallow. "How long before it begins?"

"It's hard to tell. It all depends on your body's reaction. Could be days. Could be a few weeks. Could be a couple of months. It's not something that's exactly been studied. We don't turn just anyone. In fact, there have been less than ten vampires made in the last hundred years."

"Oh, wow," I say.

"So if it helps, you should feel honored," he says, drily.

I blink at him. Was that an actual *joke?*

"Oh, one more thing," he adds. "Tomorrow, you'll be let down in the village. There is a," he waves a hand through the air, "a special event that all humans are required to attend. And since you still are, in fact, mostly human…" he shrugs, "it'll just be a formality for you to be there. You shouldn't worry."

But I don't even know what there is to be worried about.

Chapter Thirty

ELEIRA

April and I are awakened after less than six hours of sleep by a loud knocking on the door.

"I'll give you five minutes to get dressed," Raul calls from the other side. "And then I'm coming in."

She and I both scramble into our respective clothes. I put on another ridiculous dress. She gets into the peasant garb.

Raul sweeps into the room. It's the first time I've seen him in days, and my breath catches at his crisp outfit. He looks stunningly handsome and very sharp.

But he doesn't so much as glance at me. Instead, he speaks to the air. "Both of you will accompany me down to the town square," he says. "You will not speak to anyone unless given explicit permission by me. Eleira, I know you won't have any problems with that. April—you might. Lots of people down there know who you are. They've been wondering about you. Unless you want to lose your place as Eleira's favorite, and at the same time forsake my Mother's protection, you will keep your mouth shut. Understand?"

April nods.

"Hold on," I say. "You're not telling us anything. Why are we going down there, what's happening?"

He glances at me, and I can't help but suck a sharp little breath in. For a moment, I thought I glimpsed actual *fear* in his eyes.

"Nothing," he says finally. "Nothing you should worry over. It's just a formality. Nothing more."

His words remind me so much of what Phillip said last night that they all but confirm there's a secret the two brothers are keeping from me.

***

It feels ridiculously good to be let go out into nature again. But the feeling evaporates as soon as I hear and see the anxious crowd of humans buzzing in front of me.

They are gathered around a large bonfire that blazes far

above their heads. Murmurs and whispers abound. As Raul leads us to them, a nasty feeling of apprehension floats up in my gut.

"Psst," I whisper to April. "Hey, do you know what this is?"

She casts a look at Raul to see if he objects to us talking before nodding and saying, "Yeah. It's the draft."

"Draft? Draft for what?"

"Draft for the lottery, for The Hunt," she says. "They have us put our names in now, then draw them the night before."

"But we just had a full moon," I say. "Why are they doing it so early?"

"I don't know." April sounds concerned. "Usually it's a week before."

Raul glances back. "Silence!" he commands.

April and I shut our mouths.

When we walk through the villagers, a way parts for us. I hear their whispers. They're just as confused and concerned by the early gathering as April.

My stomach sinks when we stop, and I see the Queen standing triumphantly before the fire. Our eyes meet. She winks.

She addresses the crowd. "Welcome, welcome, citizens of The Haven. You know why we're gathered today. It's time for you to enter your names in the upcoming lottery!"

On her announcement, the fire behind her flares and roars.

Raul's shoulders stiffen.

"You all know the procedure," The Queen continues. "You'll be given a clay token by my guards." She motions them forward. Two vampires start distributing the coin-sized tokens from leather pouches. "Upon which you will press your thumb, thus marking it as your own. Remember, any who are caught cheating will *instantly* be sacrificed to the fire." She laughs in delight. "And you are all being watched, so don't think you're protecting a loved one by standing in for them."

The guard passes and gives me a token without looking. I cradle it in my palm.

"Does everybody have their token? Yes? Good! We will begin, oh..." she scans the crowd, and points at an elderly woman at random. "With you!"

A space instantly clears around the human, leaving her entirely on her own.

Nobody protects anybody here, I think. *Are they all so cowed?*

I watch as she approaches the fire. She walks by The Queen, who leans over and embraces her like an old friend. "What is your name?" she asks.

"S-Sally," the woman answers.

"Well, Sally," Morgan smiles. "I sincerely hope the fire does not select you." I've never heard a more false proclamation in my life. "Now go on."

The gray-haired woman nods, unsteadily, and moves closer to the flames. She takes a deep breath, closes her eyes, mutters a prayer... and throws the token in.

A horrible hissing sound comes when the token drops into the bonfire. A single dark, black wisp of smoke rises from where it fell.

"And it is done!" Morgan announced grandly. "You're free to go." She looks around the crowd. "Who's next?"

And so the ceremony continues. Each of the humans is herded to the front one-by-one. Each is given some assurance by the Queen. Then each throws their token in.

The fire takes it and spits out a black stream of smoke every single time.

Eventually it falls on me and April. The Queen looks at us, standing together. Half the crowd has already dispersed.

April starts to approach, but I pull her back. "Let me go first," I say.

She hesitates, then nods. "Okay."

Morgan fixes me with a horribly predatory look. I keep my back straight and walk toward her with dignity equal to hers.

"Good luck," she whispers as I pass.

I stop in front of the fire. I press my thumb deep into the soft underside of the token and see the mark it leaves. Then, with a quick jerk, I toss it in.

The flames cackle and hiss around it, as if the token was blown in by a great gale. For a moment the fire seems to *resist* touching the stone.

And then with a giant roar the flames sweep overtop, with all the anger of a tidal wave. My token burns.

But instead of giving out a black stream of smoke, this one is a hideous blue.

Gasps come from the crowd behind me. Even the Queen sucks in a breath.

"This one is cursed!" someone exclaims.

Commotion erupts all around me. Before I know what is happening, my arms are seized by the two guards. Angry screams come from the humans.

"Burn her!"

"She's a witch!"

"Destroy her before she can ruin us!"

They're all rallying against me, and I've never seen them joined in one cause before. I struggle and cry out and try to break free from the guards. But they are vampires, their strength is extraordinary, and I don't accomplish much.

The blue stream continues to billow out from the fire, filling the air with a poisonous smog.

"Unhand her!" Raul's voice is clear from the rest. "Don't you know who she is? Let her go!"

The guards spin me around in time for me to see Raul trying to fight through toward me. He's being restrained by the rest of the Queen's personal guards. Morgan stands a safe distance away, taking it all in.

"Did you not hear me?" Raul cries out. "I said, release her!"

The villagers beyond him continue to call for my head. Somebody grabs April and pushes her forward, then shoves her down. "She's with her!" the man who did it exclaims.

My head swivels back and forth. I can't make sense of any of it—except that something has gone wrong. Very, very wrong.

Finally the vile cries reach such a crescendo that they force Morgan to act. She throws both hands up. "Order!" she calls. "Your Queen demands order!"

She's ignored by the roiling, angry mass.

"I said, ORDER!" she exclaims. She emphasizes the command by clapping her hands together overhead. Sound like thunder crashing comes from her palms.

That sends the crowd into silence. "Well." She throws her head back, trying to regain her regal air. "That was... unexpected. A blue flame comes once every dozen years. If not less."

"It was a set up!" Raul yells. "You knew what you were doing. You set her up!"

Morgan glances at her son. She scoffs. "Please. Don't accuse me so baselessly."

The humans hang on the interaction between the vampires

with bated breath.

"You knew this would happen," Raul growls. "It is why you insisted on bringing her!"

"No," the Queen says. "I insisted on bringing her, after your riveting speech in the courtroom about following the letter of the law. Well," she shrugs. "This was it."

I can't take it anymore. "Can somebody tell me what's happening!" I scream.

The Queen's head jerks to me. "Of course." She manages to smile. "Your token flared blue. It means on the night of the next Hunt… you will be the only prey."

Chapter Thirty-One

RAUL

I storm into my Mother's chambers, anger burning in my very soul.

"How could you?" I yell at her. "How could you do that? To *her*!"

She looks up at me, as calm as if we hadn't nearly seen the beginning of a riot just minutes ago. "How could I what, sweetest?"

"Don't play games with me, woman." I slam my hand on her royal desk. "I know you rigged the lottery. You *wanted* to make an example of Eleira."

"Don't be ridiculous," she censures. "Why would I want that? Eleira is the one who is supposed to succeed me, after all."

"And yet..." I lower my tone and make it dangerous. "And yet, maybe you're not ready to give up power. Maybe you *want* to rule for another six-hundred years."

She glares at me. "Another six-hundred years of this misery? Unable to leave The Haven, unable to see the world? Always residing over the petty bickering of our people?" She scoffs. "I think not."

"Then why did you do it?" I ask. "Why did you let Eleira's token flare blue?"

"You say that as if I had any control—"

"You had *all* the control, witch!"

My temper's running away from me. I know I need to get a rein on it. But Morgan's false denials are driving me crazy.

I force my breathing to slow. "You had all the control," I repeat, "because you are the one who distributed the tokens. *You* are the one who cast the spell on them that enables them to make their selection."

"And once that spell is cast, do you think I have any further influence?" She chuckles. "No. Once the spells are unleashed they are out of my control. Blame the magic, if you will. Blame chance, blame fate. But do not blame me."

"So what now? Do you just expect me to allow you to sacrifice Eleira? After what we went through to bring her here? After all the plans we've made? We've waited *ages* for her!"

"You speak as if I have a choice." Morgan goes back to studying her reflection in the mirror. "The law is clear. Eleira must be made an example of."

Chapter Thirty-Two

ELEIRA

After the commotion at the fire, Morgan's guards dragged me away to a new series of dark, underground caves. They threw me into a tiny cell, slammed the door, and left me here without a word of explanation.

I've been here for hours and hours and hours.

The tunnels we made our way through were pitch-black. Vampires can see in the dark. They have no need for light. Myself, on the other hand...

Well, *terrified* doesn't even begin to explain my mental state.

The irony of being locked underground is not lost on me. Last time I was in a similar position, The Hunt was in full swing. I still remember the terrible screaming.

This time, *I'm* the one who's to be hunted at the next full moon.

At least, that's what my understanding of it is. There's obviously a lot which I still don't know. Would they really throw me to the wolves, after making me feel so… special?

Maybe all of it was a sham. Maybe all the preparations that were being made were just a way of fattening me up before the feast. Maybe, maybe…

The rattle of the lock catches my attention. I shy back. There's nowhere to hide. Whoever's here has definitely come for me.

The cell door creaks open. A small, flickering flame from a zippo comes to life. And then a torch is lit, and the light shows…

"Phillip!" I exclaim. I don't think I've ever been more glad to see a vampire in my life.

"I'm here to rescue you," he announces grandly. Then some of the smoke from the torch goes up his windpipe, and he starts to cough, quite violently, ruining the heroic effect.

But my joy is immediate. I fly into his arms and embrace him in a hug.

"I'm so glad to see you," I admit.

"Yes, well…" he straightens his glasses. "I wasn't there, but Raul told me what happened. It isn't right."

"Would they really do it?" I ask. "Would they make me the sole human prey in the Hunt?"

"The other vampires would have a field day with you," Phillip says. "You can't possibly know how sweet your blood smells. I'm afraid you'll never know, because there's never been another like you."

"But why?" I insist. "What's so special about *my* blood?"

"It might have something to do with The Spark," Phillip ventures. "But the reason is irrelevant. The effect you exert on others of my kind is not."

"What's the plan, then?" I ask. "What do we do now? And why—" I stop to think, "—why do you go against your own Mother, for me?"

He hesitates, clearly nervous. That's another first. I didn't think there could be such a thing as a nervous vampire.

"It was Raul's idea," he admits. "I'm just the accomplice. He's causing a distraction above ground. While that's going on, I'm supposed to whisk you to safety," he clears his throat. "Through the belly of The Catacombs."

"Is that bad?" I wonder.

"Oh no," he said dryly. "Not bad at all. Unless, of course, you happen to be frightened of legions of The Convicted, who've been locked down there without a drop of blood for, oh, let's say... two hundred years?"

A shiver crawls down my spine. I swallow.

Chapter Thirty-Three

RAUL

I lay down the last of the tinder, carefully hidden around the base of the final human home.

Then I straighten and walk away without so much as a glance back. I spot Jacob waiting for me in the trees. His wife Patricia is on the other side of the village, waiting for our signal.

The two vampires look greatly restored after having their share of blood. I mutter a quick thank you for the circumstance that brought them to me. Were it not for their help, this whole mission would be impossible.

I have friends among the other vampires, of course, but none whose loyalty can be as certain as that of these two. They owe their lives to me, after all.

I catch April's eye and give her a quick nod. The girl has steely determination plastered all over her face. When the fires start, she's the one who's going to run into the village and raise the alarm.

I look back at the quiet village. Soon, it'll all go up in flames. If there's one thing certain to destroy a vampire, it's fire. Our kind will do all that they can to avoid the deadly flames. However, once the conflagration rises, its size and scope will draw all of them to put it out.

I only hope there won't be many human casualties in the fire. I made sure to leave them scattered escape routes throughout the village. Not too obvious, because I don't want this linked back to me—I want to make this look as natural as possible. But not too difficult to see in the panic either.

"Are you sure about this, my Prince?" Jacob asks me when I join him in our hideout.

"Yes," I say. There is not a shred of hesitation in my answer. "Mother started her games with the draft bonfire. Well, the best way to fight fire is *with* fire."

Chapter Thirty-Four

ELEIRA

"Wait." Phillip holds an arm out and stops me in my tracks. "Wait, I think I hear someone up ahead."

My breath catches, and I stop. I strain my ears for any sound. I hear nothing.

"Never mind." Phillip says after a tense moment. "It's nothing. Maybe a bat."

I exhale.

We've been navigating the underground tunnels for what feels like days. Phillip asked me if he could put the torch out. He said it hurt his eyesight more than it helped mine. I didn't like the idea of being cast in total darkness, but I liked the idea of being discovered even less.

So I agreed.

"Let's go," he says. I cling to his arm. He murmurs directions under his breath.

"There's a downslope here."

"We're turning left now."

"Watch out, the ground is rocky."

And so on and so forth.

I follow him without a single word of protest. Somehow, two of the three vampires who were responsible for my abduction have now crossed over to my side.

Who'd have thought that would happen when I woke up in the atrium?

But I can't keep quiet forever. Uncertainty is eating me up inside.

Eventually, I whisper, "Where are we going? Where are you leading me?"

"I'm taking you out of The Haven," Phillip says. "We have to go beneath the wards erected above us. It's the only way to bypass them."

For a moment I'm too stunned to offer a credible response. "You're actually... helping me *escape* this place? Not just the dungeon?"

"It wouldn't do you much good if I took you out of your cell and brought you back amongst vampires, would it?" he asks. "Besides," he tugs me forward, "this was all Raul's idea. Like I said."

I can't help the smile that comes from his words. It may have been Raul's idea, but Phillip wouldn't be cooperating without his consent.

"Thank you," I say. "From the bottom of my heart... thank you."

"Don't thank me yet," Phillip warns. "We still haven't reached the most treacherous part. The Convicted are going to be our greatest challenge."

I stop short. "You mean... I thought you were leading us around them."

"Oh no," Phillip gives a soft laugh. "There is no going around where they are. It's through them, and then to the Outside. From there... Raul will meet you. You'll go with him."

I clear my throat. I feel Phillip look at me. "Do you have a problem with that?"

Not exactly, I think. It's just that he and I haven't had a proper conversation since sharing that chaste kiss. Not about *us*, or what the kiss meant, anyway.

If it meant anything at all. I could be reading too much into things.

"No problem," I blurt out.

"Are you sure?" Phillip questions. "If you prefer, we could always turn back…"

His dry tone tells me it's another joke. Just like his previous one, it falls flat.

"So what are the Convicted, anyway?" I ask after we move on.

"If you've ever seen one of them, you'd know. They're these… creatures who "

"I *have* seen them," I interrupt. "One attacked me during The Hunt. Your brother saved me from it."

Phillip spins around. "*What?*" he exclaims.

"April and I were being held underground. A tall man in a red coat appeared. He had no teeth. Only fangs. And his tongue… I think his tongue was cut out."

"Cut out and denied from growing back by Mother's spell," Phillip murmurs. "I had no idea that happened to you. Raul saved you? But, how could the Convicted have reached you? I know where you were kept, there's no way…" he trails off.

"Unless," he said, "*unless,* somebody released him. Well — released *it.* Those creatures have no gender. Another thing that Mother takes away."

I swallow in discomfort.

"They are — were — once vampires," Phillip says. "They were the ones found guilty of crimes against others of our kind. That is why they suffer the worst punishment. Their tongues are removed. They are given no blood. They are locked deep underground, where they can never see the moon or the stars. Even vampires have the need for freedom. Moonlight invigorates us. The Convicted are locked away underground. For life. Until they meet their end."

"I thought vampires are immortal?" I ask.

"In a way. Our spirits linger. But our bodies can decompose. It takes years—decades, centuries, of absolute misery. We don't do anything to their teeth—they fall out on their own to make room for their fangs... fangs which continue to grow longer and longer, because they're starved for blood.

"They lose all of their humanity down there. They become horrible, awful, creatures, driven only by their basest instinct — the one for blood."

"You torture them," I breathe.

"Not directly," Phillip says. "But it's not a pleasant existence, to say the least. Maybe *you* would have been able to influence things, had this latest wrinkle not occurred."

"I'm not going to be welcomed back after this escape, am I?"

"I was going to say, we have to succeed first. But your point is valid. You won't be welcomed back… as a human."

Chapter Thirty-Five

RAUL

The fire started innocently enough, but soon grew way out of control. I was too eager with setting the dry hay. I'd used too much, and now the conflagration is threatening the entirety of The Haven.

Screams and shouts surround me.

I race from my kind to the humans, risking my own life to pull them from their burning homes. Only a handful of other vampires are doing the same. Most are concerned with putting out the flames. There is no love lost between our species. Most of the vampires who *could* help, chose to look out for their own skin.

I'm no saint, but for now, I'm different. The fire was *my* idea. I feel acutely responsible for every human life that might be lost. The more I can do to reduce casualties, the better it will be.

Besides, I have Patricia watching out for Eleira's emergence. Once the girl appears, I'm gone.

"We need more water!" April screams. The humans have formed a bucket line and are passing on pails from the nearest lake. I curse my Mother's insistence in not providing the village modern technologies. This would be so much simpler if we had a hose.

But then again, this way, Eleira has more time to escape.

I run back into the flames engulfing the village, searching, searching, always searching for more humans who need my help. My attention goes to a tiny hut. My vampire senses tell me there are people inside.

I crash through the doors. Two children are huddling in a corner. A burning pillar separates me from them.

They're crying for their mother. I look around—and my heart sinks when I find her trapped beneath the pillar.

I run over and strain to pick it up. "Please, no," the woman pleads. She has eyes only for her children. "Save them. Not me. Please!"

I have enough time to do both — but then I understand. The way the woman's back is twisted, it's been broken.

She won't walk again.

And in The Haven, a cripple's life lasts only until the next Hunt.

"I'm sorry," I whisper, and jump the burning beam to grab her two children. They scream for her and beat against my back. I clutch them to me and pull them out of the burning building.

Seconds after we emerge, a great crash sounds behind us. A blast of hot air whips against my body. I don't need to look to know the roof had caved in. The cries of the children are evidence enough.

I race to a safe clearing some distance away from the fire. The younger humans are gathered there. "Somebody look after them!" I command as I set the children down. Then, knowing they're finally safe, I turn back and run straight into the fires.

Over and over I repeat the process, hunting down the people trapped inside, pulling them out, dragging them to safety. Most are too hysterical to notice who I am. The ones who do, look at me look in wonder. *Why would the Prince risk himself for us?*

But they've only seen the side of vampires that Mother has allowed them to see. They don't know, cannot fathom, that beyond our need for blood, we're a lot like them. We *were* them, once, and just because we've transformed, does not mean we've become creatures with different needs, desires, wants, doubts, and, yes, even insecurities, as when we were human.

Of course, it's hard to imagine those *human* qualities in a race that keeps you constantly oppressed.

On and on it goes. I catch glimpses of other vampires darting through the flames. I wish I could say they were there rescuing the trapped humans, but I know better than that. The truth is, most are probably taking advantage of the confusion to feed.

I run back to the outskirts. I call for my Mother, the Queen. I don't spot her anywhere, but surely she knows what's happening.

"Where is the Queen?" I demand of the vampire nearest to me. "Where is your monarch?"

"She hasn't been seen, my Lord," he answers quickly. "It's just been us."

"And her guards? Have they come?"

He shakes his head. "No."

I curse. I should have known better than to expect Mother to risk her personal guard for the sake of the villagers, but if they're not here, it means she could have sent them to ensure Eleira doesn't escape.

I curse again. I just pray Phillip has enough luck on his side.

"Raul! Raul!"

April is screaming my name. I run to her. She's taking care of the children that have been separated from their parents.

"What is it?"

"Raul, you *have* to go!" Her eyes latch onto mine. "You've wasted too much time. Most of the villagers are safe. We'll get the rest. Go!"

I know she's speaking the truth. But my conscience won't let me just abandon the humans I've condemned.

"Patricia?" I ask. "Jacob? Where are they?"

"Already gone! They're waiting for you. We'll manage. Go!"

I can't believe the earnestness in the girl's voice. Does she really care so much for Eleira?

"Yes," I say grimly. "Yes, you're right. I'll —"

A terrible scream sounds from the very heart of the village. The fire is still raging there.

My head whips around. "What was that?"

"What? Raul, you have to —"

But of course the girl couldn't have picked out the sound. Not amongst the chaos raging all around us.

I take off without another word. The scream comes again, and it's so shrill, so filled with fear, that I cannot just ignore it.

It's like the screams that come the night of The Hunt.

I see a farmhouse in the middle. The entire structure is engulfed in flames. The screaming is coming from inside.

I dart around the building, searching for a safe way in. The heat beats against my skin. It's like being caught in the middle of an inferno. I see the safe path out, the one I'd laid out beforehand. All I need to do is get whoever is inside out of the farmhouse and put them on the path. Then I can go to Eleira.

There's no easy way in. So I resort to using brute force. I shield my face with one arm and barrel into the main doors. They split then fall, the timbers weakened by the flames.

Inside, I discover a horrific sight.

There's a group of humans bound to a central beam like hostages in a robbery. Eleven of them. They have rags stuffed into their mouths to prevent them from yelling. Nearby, a group of four vampires are throwing a half-naked woman between themselves. She's alive, but her body is marred by bite marks. On her chest, her arms, her back, her neck. Her ripped dress is stained with blood.

The vampires are too preoccupied with their little game to notice me. They're too far caught up in their bloodlust.

One of them catches the screaming woman and sinks his fangs into her neck. He drinks and he lets her go, then pushes her to his accomplice, who catches her and takes his fill.

She isn't the first they've done this to. There are three discarded bodies on the dirt floor.

They were the ones who screamed for help.

Such anger fills me at the display. A horrible fount of rage opens up inside me. I know the four vampires. They're part of my Mother's guard.

I step forward. The bound humans have seen me. But they think I'm the next of their torturers, so they huddle back in fright.

"Stop!" I command. "In the name of the Queen's rule, stop what you are doing!"

My voice echoed around the room. The vampires turn their heads to me. Their eyes are glazed over in ecstasy. They've consumed more than their fair share of blood. Much, much more —

so much as to make them lazy. The feast has turned them into drunkards.

"Oh," one of them says. He drops the woman, who crumbles to the floor. "Look who it is. The Prince."

He takes an unsteady step toward me. His body lurches one way before he catches himself. He gives a mocking bow.

"Won't you join us, your Highness?" He swings an arm to the captives. "Their blood is fresh and yours for the taking."

I know this man specifically. He's Andrey, one of James's closest confidants, and also his gambling pal.

"You know the law," I snarl. I take an aggressive step toward him. "No humans are to be taken except in The Hunt, or by special decree."

"Decree? Decree, you say?" His three friends stare at me, their jaws slack like junkies who've just had their hit. Andrey's hand juts into his coat pocket. "Well, I've got your decree right here..."

For a second my heart stops beating. *Could Mother have actually sanctioned this?*

But then Andrey's hand comes back out holding with nothing but a finger raised in obscene gesture toward me.

"There's your damn decree, *Prince*," he spits. "We all know James is the heir to the throne. Not you."

He laughs, and his cronies join in.

By now, my blood is boiling. "You've taken this a step too far," I threaten.

"Oh, really?" He motions for his friends to join him. They form a solid wall separating me from the humans. The poor woman they were taking advantage of lies in a heap on the ground, barely even breathing. "And what are you going to do? *Convict* us? We all saw what you did in the court." He jabs a finger into my chest. "We know what a stickler for the *rules* you are."

The last insult is too much. They may be the Queen's guards but I am Raul Soren. Only two vampires in the coven stand above me; my Mother and James. Only the former is stronger than I am.

"I'm going to say this one more time." My voice comes in a soft growl. "Let. The humans. Go."

Andrey puffs up. "Is that a threat?"

"You bet your bloodthirsty heart it is." I address the others from his gang. "Let the human go, leave now, and no chargers will be laid."

Andrey scoffs. "And if we refuse? It's four against one, Prince."

"If you refuse," my tone becomes dangerous. "I will have no choice but to kill you."

Andrey's expression changes to one of shock, and then a split-second later, stark anger. His face screws up, and his claws jut out as he lunges at me.

But I'm faster than he is. I duck around and come up behind him, then strike him in the back of his neck. It's a debilitating blow. I feel his spine fracture beneath my hand. He goes down—but then the others are on me.

They crash into me, snarling, swiping, biting, fangs and claws out. For a moment I'm at the bottom of the heap. Then, with a savage roar, I surge up and throw the three vampires off.

They recover fast. Now they know I'm a threat. My eyes flash to the humans, who are paralyzed by fear and shock—and wonder. They're astounded that I would stand up for them, just like the villagers who recognized me earlier were astounded I was risking my life to get them to safety.

The vampire on my right throws himself at me. His claws

scrape along my chest, cutting through the clothes and gouging deep into my skin. But his attack leaves his throat exposed. I roll with him, using his momentum to carry us to the side. My hand clasps onto his Adam's apple, and I crush his windpipe. He falls, and then there are only two left.

They look to each other, no longer so certain of themselves. Their eyes connect, and they give the most minuscule of nods. They're going to come at me together, and I no longer have the element of surprise.

The muffled cries of the humans continue in the background. From the corner of my vision I see the bloodied woman crawling toward them, using the last of her strength to work on the knot in the heavy rope around them all.

In that moment I have the utmost admiration for her.

Then the two guards fly at me, and I'm consumed by the fight. I see a flash of silver in one of their hands. I don't have time to react to it before the knife is thrust into my thigh.

I cry out, then roar in anger. I rip the weapon free, twist, and impale it into the vampire's heart. He didn't expect me to move so fast. His eyes widen in shock, and then he collapses.

Now it's just me and one other. The cut along my chest is already closing. But the healing process is making me thirst for blood. The scent of blood from the woman, even from the human corpses, becomes incredibly tantalizing. I was able to ignore it before, but now...

My drop of focus gives the last guard the opening he needs. He ducks his shoulder and slams into me, catching me in the midriff. We crash into a burning wooden beam. The impact makes it crack and splinter. I hear a heavy groan, and then part of the roof collapses beyond us.

Suddenly the humans are trapped. Fire rages on all sides. The air, already thick, is filling more and more with smoke. Some of it escapes from the new hole in the ceiling, but most of it builds and builds from the burning timber close to the ground.

I fend off the vampire's claws and struggle against him. He smells the human blood, too, but now his eyes are set on a much more lucrative feast:

The blood of his Prince.

He pulls back his lips, and his fangs extend. I catch him by his jaw just inches from my neck. The venom drips from the points. It takes all my fading strength to keep him off me, my mind is still being pulled in two directions with the bloodlust on one side and the need to fight on the other.

His jaw snaps, and his hands grip my shoulders. His claws sink into me. I scream in pain. I focus only on keeping him off.

Suddenly there's a cry of euphoria and a rush of movement on the other side of the farm. The woman's managed to set the humans free. They don't have an escape, but they still lumber away from the fight, away from the blasting fire.

At the same time, a draft of wind sweeps from the hole in the roof. It blows the scent of the humans away and gives me just the opportunity I needed to refocus my attention.

My hands split between my body and that of the guard's. I pare them apart and shove the guard off me. I have the briefest moment to lunge at him, extending my own claws to sink them through his chest.

They find his heart.

He looks at me in wonder... and then dies.

I gasp for breath. I'm heaving with exhaustion. I've just killed four of my own kind. None of the Convicted have committed crimes greater than that.

Not even close.

But I don't have time to reflect on my sins. The barn is going up in flames. It's becoming more and more dangerous by the second.

I need to get the humans out. I scan the surroundings. There's no way for them to escape without going through the burning part of the roof that's now on the ground. And that's impossible.

My own way out, from the other side, is clear. The roof groans and the fire licks the base of the walls. I turn to escape. Anguished cries call for me from the other side. They think I'm going to abandon them.

"I'll be back!" I scream. "Stay away from the wall! As far away as you can get. Do it now!"

They huddle together, panicking, and seem incapable of following my instructions.

"Now!" I command.

Then another pillar collapses and I lose sight of the group. I rip back and jump through the flame to get outside. Adrenaline is pumping through my body. I don't know what else would compel me to act so rashly this close to fire.

But the humans — they need to be saved.

In the deep of the night I am the only one present. The homes around me are all evacuated. Each one still billows and smokes. I run to the part of the barn where the humans are. I look for something I can use to break the wall in. But all I have are my bare hands.

"I can't believe I'm going to do this." I mutter an oath, close my eyes, and use all the force I can to slam my body into the building.

I crash through the wall into a fiery hell. The humans see me and cry out in surprise.

"Go!" I scream at them. "Go, now!"

They rush past me to safety.

I'm about to turn back—when that tantalizing blood scent catches my attention again.

The woman who saved them is still inside.

I run through the interior, searching for her. I know I have only seconds left. The structure will soon give way, and when it falls, there'll be no escape. I'll surely die, and, even worse—I'll have failed Eleira.

But something in my conscience prevents me from leaving

the woman to her fate.

I spot her right where she fell after untying the knot. I leap past the flames and cradle her in my arms. The smell of her blood is overwhelming, enticing, exotic. It's all I can do not to sink my fangs into her and draw deep. My body needs it, the monster inside me craves it, and the bloodlust is infinitely close to consuming me whole.

But I fight it off. I fight it all off and think only of Eleira and my need to get to her.

This woman barely has any life left. Her eyes are closed, her heart is weakly beating. I can feel her fading away. I navigate the obstacles left in my path and emerge on the outside. The humans I released have already scattered. I start to run, getting as far away from the fires as possible.

I reach the edge of the woods. Heat from the fire still blazes, but it's so much cooler here in contrast.

I set the woman down gently on the forest floor. She doesn't stir. The bite marks over her body are horrendous. Her dress is ripped, and she takes the most feeble, shallow breaths. They sound faint even to my inhumanly vampire hearing.

She's only got minutes to cling onto life. Maybe less. The

scope of my failure consumes me. Who is this woman, this *human*, to me? Nobody. And yet, I feel compelled to help. Not just because of my guilt for causing all this. No, it goes deeper than that.

I want to help because Eleira woke something up inside me, something that has lain latent since Liana's death.

Compassion, or at least a renunciation of the stark indifference that has lain heavily over my heart for centuries.

I look around. There's nobody near us. I open my senses to the world.

Still nothing. The woman and I are completely alone.

I look at my wrist. I see the vein pulsing on the underside. There is only one thing that will grant the woman life—one thing that has been forbidden by the highest rescript of The Haven's law.

I have no choice. I bring my wrist to my mouth. My fangs extend. I puncture the skin.

A fount of blood flows out.

I press it to the woman's lips. "Drink," I tell her. I tilt her head back. "Drink, and be well."

The first drops hit her tongue. Her body seizes. I pinch her nose to get her to swallow. It's a vile trick that I'm doing, but it truly is the only way.

When the first bit of blood reaches the back of her throat she gasps. She starts to cough. I continue to press my wrist to her. She needs all the blood she can get. Her system will reject it at the start, but when the healing starts, she won't be able to get enough.

That will be the most dangerous part for both of us.

Little by little she draws it in. Her heartbeat strengthens. Her breathing steadies. A flush enters her cheeks, and then, slowly, the wounds on her body begin to close.

Suddenly her eyes pop open. Her hands jut out and she grabs my arm. She starts to suck for all she's worth. I feel her draining me, and I let her, but the balance has to be absolutely precise —

She's had enough. I rip my arm free. She snarls, consumed by a distant version of the bloodlust we vampires feel.

I pin her down and she fights for more. Her body's been revitalized. But her mind is not currently hers. She's operating on base instinct, the instinct that my blood has engaged in her.

"*No!*" I say. "No, there is no more!"

He lips draw back in anger. If she'd been converted her fangs would have flashed. But she's only human, and currently harmless.

The danger comes from within me.

Because now, with her body healing, and *my* body drained, the dynamic has shifted. *I* need her blood. I need it badly. She reeks of it: hot, full, florid, fresh. My own instincts are fighting with me to draw on her. She's whole, she's available, she's caught beneath me. And the way she's struggling against my hold makes it so much more enticing. She is prey caught in the hunter's snare. Every time she thrashes about, I'm only reminded more of her vitality and of my own need to *steal* it from her.

With a grunt I push off. I'm on my feet in an instant and fly back against the nearest tree. My nostrils flare. Every cell in my body is crying out to take the woman's life. Every cell...

And then she looks at me and blinks a few times in recognition and she... she starts to cry.

I grip the tree trunk. I can't let go for fear that if I do, I'll lose control and pounce on her.

"What — why are you crying?" I force the words out, each one needed to distract me from what I really want to do.

"You," she says. "It's you. They said you'd come."

I shake my head. That doesn't make any sense. "*Who* said I'd come?"

"The other vampires. They — they used me. They said I was bait, to bring you there."

"The other vampires are dead," I tell her firmly.

She gasps. "What?"

"I killed them. I saw what they were doing to you."

She looks down at herself. She shakes her head in remembrance. "But... I'm alive? How?"

"I fed you my blood," I rasp. I draw my fingers in deeper so I don't break away. "You humans don't know this, but a vampire's blood can heal. Mine, most of all."

"Why would you do that?" She's composed herself enough so the tears are no longer flowing.

"You would have died without it."

"You would... kill four vampires, just to rescue one human?"

"I owed it to you. You freed the rest."

"But they —"

"Got out safely," I finish for her. "You know where you are? You know the path back?"

She looks around, considers, and nods. "I can find my way."

"Then go," I say. "Go before I do something I'll regret."

"Like what?" she begins.

"GO!" I roar.

She stumbles up. I cannot contain the bloodlust for much longer.

"NOW!" I scream.

She cries out, frightened, and then runs past me.

Only when her footsteps fade completely from hearing do I ease my death grip from the tree and stagger toward the rendezvous point with Phillip and Eleira.

Chapter Thirty-Six

ELEIRA

I creep after Phillip, his cold hand clasped around my warm one like a lifeline.

He's forbidden me from speaking. He's taken us deeper and deeper into the earth, where he said we were closing in on our escape route. The one that takes us through the den of The Convicted.

After we travel down for what seems an age, we reach an enormous iron gate. There are torches lit around it. Phillip holds a finger to his lips to signal for silence and points for me to stay. Then he approaches it on his own.

No sooner does he come within five feet of it than the low, horrible moan of a Convicted comes from the other side. I can barely stop from crying out in pain as I clasp my hand over my ears. The first moan is followed by a second, then a third, and suddenly, all three Convicted appear on the other side, hands stretching out through the bars, grasping for Phillip.

He jumps back to me. Needless to say, we can't take that route. So he leads me another way, telling me there are a variety of other passages we can try.

He doesn't sound exactly certain when he admits that. So it doesn't do wonders for my confidence.

Suddenly, he stops. I'm so absorbed in my thoughts that I bump into him.

"What happened?" I whisper, before remembering myself and clamping a hand over my mouth.

"I think..." he says slowly. "I think we're being followed."

"What!"

"Shh!"

"By whom?"

"I'm not sure," he tells me. "It couldn't be another Convicted. They're all on the other side."

"A vampire?" I breathe.

"If it were, I don't think we'd have gotten this far. We need to be more careful."

I mutter something about that being close to impossible after how careful we've already been.

"Just keep your ears open," Phillip snaps, and we continue on.

Yeah, like that would help, I think. You're the one with preternatural hearing.

We keep on through the darkness. The raw smell of the earth surrounds me. It's dank and heavy and oppressive.

After Phillip's warning I can't help but feel on edge. Even though I've got a vampire companion, I'm frightened of what might be after us.

We reach a small tunnel. "We'll have to go through," Phillip says. "Careful, I know you can't see. You need to crawl."

"Okay," I nod. I feel the shape of the entrance with my hands. Its top is only halfway up to my waist. Otherwise it's barely wider than my shoulders. "Are we close? What's on the other side?"

The anticipation is killing me.

"The den," Phillip tells me. "Come on."

I swallow my fear, drop to my knees, and crawl in.

My body scrapes against the rock. There's a tiny stream of water running along the ground. My hands splash in it and get dirty.

Far ahead I see a dim blue light. My breath catches, and my heart begins beating with hope. Phillip moves faster, and it's such a relief to be able to finally *see* the outline of his body and know that he is, in fact, there in front of me.

But as we keep going, I find there is no opening. There *is* no source of light.

Suddenly, I remember what I was told about the transformation. *The eyes are the first to change.*

I let on a tiny cry of alarm. Phillip jerks his head back. "What?"

"I think... I think I can see you." I blink, and he becomes clearer to me in the black. "Oh *yes.* I definitely see you."

"The transformation," he murmurs.

I swallow. "What's going to happen to me?"

"For now? That is it. But we need to move faster. Raul wants you to be clear out of The Haven when it begins."

"Why?"

Phillip doesn't answer. Instead, he turns and continues to crawl.

"I said, why?" I exclaim.

"I don't want to fill your head with worries," he mutters. "Not now."

"Oh yeah, as if I don't have any of those right now," I fire back.

"Exactly," he says. "Why add to the mix? Let's focus on getting out of here safely. Although I will tell you this. It's going to be a lot easier for us to get through now that you can see."

***

We emerge into a narrow opening running between two tall cliffs. Looking up, I think I can see parts of the top of the cave. But it could just be my imagination. We still have a long way to go.

"We're here," Phillip says.

"Where? In the den?" I shiver. "That means any of The Convicted can just find us."

"Not if we take the proper precautions."

"Like what?"

"Staying quiet." He gives me a keen look. "Not asking too many questions. Following my lead."

"All right, all right, jeez," I mutter. "I get the point."

He flashes a rare grin. "But I do have a good feeling about this."

"Do you?"

"Yes. Let's go."

We continue sneaking through the underground. I'd hoped my vision would continue to improve in the night, but it seems stuck.

Still, *some* improvement is better than none.

We go on and on until the cave starts to expand on either side of us. It grows into a subterranean valley the size of a football stadium. We walk through it until we reach *another* opening.

The path dips down. Up ahead, there's an enormous cavern. Jagged rock makes up the cliff faces on either side.

Phillip motions for me to stop. "There," he points. "Do you see that gap, up on the far wall?"

My eyes search the rock. I pick out the tiniest flyspeck of light, at the very top of the distant surface. It's very, very high.

"What about it?" I ask.

"That's our ticket out."

"But... that's impossible. How to do we reach it? We'd have to scale the wall!" I gulp. "I'm no rock climber."

"You cling to my back, and I'll carry you," he says. He takes a deep breath. "But as soon as we enter the lower valley, every Convicted will know we're here."

"Where are they now?" I whisper.

He closes his eyes and concentrates. Then he opens them again. "I can't feel them," he admits. "But that doesn't mean they won't come fast."

"If that's the way out, why don't *they* just take it? Why don't *they* just escape?"

"More wards," Phillip explains. "Cast specifically for The Convicted. They don't know the passage exists."

"Then... who's it for? Is this how all vampires get out of The Haven?"

"No." Phillip sounds irritated. I think he's just as much on edge as I am. "We're only taking this way because you're still human. At least — in part. And this is a secret route, known only to a select few."

"You and your brothers," I guess.

"Amongst others of our royalty." He turns his back to me. "Climb on."

I wrap my arms around his neck and my legs around his torso. "I hope you know what you're doing."

"So do I," he mutters.

"That's not exactly reassuring."

"Wasn't meant to be." He grunts and repositions me on his back. "Ready?"

"As ready as I'll ever be. Yeah."

"Then let's do it."

A rush of air whistles by my ears as Phillip races forward. My hair flies back. The speed he moves with is astonishing, even frightening. Everything becomes a blur. I feel like I'm strapped to the back of a motorcycle going 300 miles an hour down a narrow street.

Suddenly something slams into me, and I'm thrown right off. I fly back through the air and hit the ground hard. Pain explodes all over my body, from my legs to my hips to my back.

Phillip jerks to a stop. "No!" he gasps.

I groan in agony. I don't think anything is broken, but I'm definitely going to be tender.

He runs back to me. "Are you all right?" he presses.

"I... I think so," I mutter. I push myself up and bring a hand to my head. There are stars in my vision. I try to steady myself...

That's when I notice a long, nasty scrape along my forearm.

Alarm rips through me. *Blood!* The Convicted, they're going to be drawn to it.

Just then, that awful moaning sound comes from the deeper reaches of the cave behind us.

"No, no, no!" Phillip curses, as I slam my hands over my ears. Their moans are echoed by my own, both from the pain in my head and the pain in my body.

"Hurry, hurry," he says, lifting me up. "We have to run!"

I hobble upright and cling on to him. But my muscles feel week, and my body still is in shock. I don't think I'll be able to hold on properly.

I don't get time to make any other decision, because right then a red-jacketed monster emerges from a far opening.

Phillip grabs my hands and forces them around his neck. We take off again, but right at the point where I flew off last time, he stops.

I look back. The moaning Convicted is coming at us, eyes glazed over, fangs gleaming, claws extended.

"The ward must be leaking through from above ground," Phillip says. "That's what threw you off me. It's like an invisible wall."

"What!" I exclaim. The deprived vampire zombie is getting closer. From other parts of the cavern, I hear his friends.

"I don't know where to go!" Phillip exclaims. He sets me down. He faces the first Convicted. "I'll buy you as much time as I can."

"What do you want me to do?" Panic is streaming through me and taking over all my thoughts. "Phillip!"

"Find a way through," he tells me. He points to either side. "The ward above ground extends horizontally like a solid wall. I did not think the magic was strong enough to reach all the way down here. But," he grunts, "it has. Yet it can't be at full strength! You need to search it for an opening, a gap, somewhere you can push through."

My heart starts pounding even faster. He wants me to find a way through an *invisible* wall?

"Go!" he exclaims. "Do it, do it now!"

And then he takes off for the nearest Convicted. I turn away immediately. I don't need to see more gore, more bloodshed.

Sounds of the fight reach my ears. I do my best to ignore it. From the distance, the moans still come. They do something to my brain, making it feel like it's being pressed together by a vice, but the effect is less than before.

Because the transformation has started?

I don't have time to consider. I run forward, fighting through the pain of my injuries, and stick my hands out to feel the wall. It's like a barrier of solid air, like a force field.

I go from side to side, desperately searching. My hands seek any weak point. But all they find is that impenetrable, smooth surface.

It feels like glass beneath my palms. I marvel that something like this is actually possible.

A scream comes from behind me. My head snaps back. I see Phillip with his hands on his knees, breathing hard.

He's leaning over the fallen body of a Convicted. The monster's heart is lying on the ground, just inches away.

I have the unquenchable urge to vomit. My stomach dry-heaves. Thank Heavens there's no food in it, or else I'd make a mess all over the floor.

There's a sound beyond him. A group of three more Convicted appear.

"Hurry!" Phillip screams.

I turn back and continue my task. But no matter where I push, no matter how I press, there's no give. Not a crack, not a gap, not an opening.

Nothing!

My breathing quickens. Panic and fear and the imminent sense of failure consume me. Desperately I run this way then that, feeling at the invisible wall with my hands.

There's no way, I think. *There's no way through!*

I chance a glance back. The horde of three is getting closer. Phillip picks up the heart and chucks it at them.

Immediately, they clamor for it, hungry and thirsting for blood. They start to fight amongst themselves, scratching and clawing and pushing one another out of the way.

"Anything?" Phillip yells.

"No!" I exclaim. Darkness starts to well in from the corners of my vision. It's the darkness of despair. *How can this be happening? We're so close, we've almost made it. I can see our escape just ahead of us.*

Phillip runs to me. "I can't fight all three," he says. He looks back the way we came. "Our only chance now is if we make a run for it. The Convicted are consumed in their battle for the heart. I'm sure it's only a temporary distraction. When they realize again that they have two victims in easy vicinity it'll all be over."

"What about The Hunt?" I say. "If we go back —"

"I'm not leading you back to The Haven. We'll look for another way out."

My eyes go to the gap in the cliff so close to us. "There is no other way out." My anguish threatens to sink me. I feel like I'm on the verge of hysteria, facing certain death. "You said it yourself; this is the secret route."

"Yes, but —" Suddenly, he cuts off. He looks up.

"Raul!" he exclaims.

"What?" Then I look at the opening, and, sure enough, I see his familiar male form.

"What's he doing here?"

"He's come for us!"

Raul is at the opening. He hangs onto the edge of the cliff and drops down. His body flows through the air like an Olympic diver's. I gasp, but he lands softly enough.

As soon as he's there, he urges us forward. "Come on, what are you doing? Hurry!"

"The ward is up!" Phillip yells. "Eloira can't get through!"

I feel so helpless, so utterly useless, so frighteningly *dependent.*

"No!" Raul runs to us. My stupid heart skips a beat when he gets close.

He passes through the wall as if it doesn't exist. Which, for him, it doesn't. He clasps his brother by the arms, then he turns to me. There's a split-second hesitation, and then he embraces me tightly.

"I'm so glad you're alive," he whispers in my ear.

He is?

"Why do you smell like smoke?" I ask.

"Long story." He lets go and looks at the three Convicted. "Are there more?"

"Not yet," Phillip says.

Raul nods. "You help Eleira. I'll take care of them."

And then, without waiting for our consent, he launches himself right at the pack.

Phillip looks from me to his brother. "He wants me to help, but I can't sense the ward..." he begins.

"I know." A sinking feeling rises in my gut. *It's all on me.*

"But maybe I can help." He hooks an arm under my shoulder and lifts me off my feet. "Put your hand out," he tells me. "I'll run back and forth and you can look for an opening that way. If any of The Convicted get through Raul, I can outrun them."

"What about —"

Raul. I want to say, but then his roar rocks the cave. I look and see him standing in the middle of three mangled bodies.

All The Convicted are dead.

He races to us. "More are coming," he says. "I can hear them."

Phillip nods. "So can I."

"How did you do that?" I blurt out. "How did you kill them so fast?"

Raul grunts. "They're weak." His eyes look haunted. I want him to extrapolate on that, but I know he won't.

Then he realizes something. "You can *see* them?" he asks, a note of alarm in his voice.

"Her transformation has begun," Phillip explains.

"Then the ward shouldn't be stopping her!" Raul says. "Right?"

"It will while she's partially human," Phillip says.

Raul slams a fist into his open hand in frustration.

A chorus of low, distant moans sounds from the far, distant reaches behind us.

We all whip around.

"They're almost here," Phillip says.

"How many are there?" I gasp.

Raul looks at his brother. "Dozens," he says. He looks at me. "And I won't be able to fight all of them off."

Chapter Thirty-Seven

RAUL

I stand with my feet spread wide, facing the opening from which The Convicted will attack.

I'm under no illusions that I can win this fight. The first three I fought were stupid and distracted by their inner battle over the heart.

Eleira's blood scent is strong in the air. It's tantalizingly human. It calls to me, and the call is only magnified to the poor monsters sentenced to waste their lives underground.

It occurs to me that I am bound to become one of them, after the murder of four of my kind.

Time for those worries later. Right now, the priority is Eleira.

She's rushing back and forth along the invisible wall with Phillip. I curse myself for my stupidity. I should have brought someone else here first, some other human, who could have served as a test-run for this.

But I acted on impulse. All I knew was that I had to get Eleira out. I couldn't let her die in The Hunt.

Except now, because of my own stupidity, she might die at the hands of these vampire ghouls.

Well, not if I can stop it. I don't care what happens to me. My life in The Haven is already forfeit. But if I can give Eleira the tiniest scrap of extra time…

I glance back at her. She doesn't know I'm looking. For a split-second I get a vision of Liana. My heart beats three times faster. It's ludicrous, the extent of control she exhibits over me.

And she doesn't even know a tenth of it.

A scraping sounds from the front. I turn my attention forward.

The first of The Convicted is there.

Instinct takes me. I fly over the ground and attack the monster. His flesh is weak. It doesn't take long for me to find the opening I need to rip his heart out.

I crush it to make sure he won't revive and throw the body down the tunnel. The Convicted rarely turn upon each other. But if the kill is certain…

Well, I've already guaranteed that. Hopefully this new quarry can distract the rest of them from Eleira's blood.

I hear a cheer of excitement behind me. "Raul!"

I whip back and discover Eleira calling me closer. I rush to her. Phillip is at her side.

"We found it!" she exclaims.

"What? An opening?"

"Yes, but we need your help."

"Anything."

Phillip's lips tighten to form a thin line. "What is it?" I ask him. "What's wrong?"

"Nothing," he says, too quickly.

"Phillip. I know you. Tell me what's wrong."

"It's not *precisely* an opening," he admits. "Eleira thinks she senses a weakness in the ward."

"Yes, yes, right here!" she exclaims. She sticks her arms out. She looks like a mime pretending to be trapped in a glass box. "It *is* weaker. Look!"

She pushes, and with a grunt, one of her arms falls through.

She pulls it back out. "But I don't have enough strength to break through myself."

"You want me to do... what exactly?"

"Get me through!"

"It'll crush her," Phillip says.

"Not if we move with great speed." She backs away. "We need as much propulsion as we can get."

She looks at me. "Carry me. Get a running start. Take me through the ward with you. But we have to go *right* here."

She outlines the spot again.

"Eleira... if you're wrong, you'll be crushed." My ears pick up the fast-approaching mass of Convicted. I shake my head. "I won't do it."

"It's the only way!" she says. "Don't think, just do it!"

"If something happens to you —"

"It's going to happen anyway with those half-dead vampires coming at us." She leans into my arms. "Now do it!"

I can't lie. Her spunk is undeniable, as is her courage. I don't know how she's changed so much in her short time in The Haven, but she's grown, gotten bolder.

Other girls might wilt in her position. Not Eleira.

She reminds me of Liana more and more.

I nod. "Phillip?"

"Be careful with her," he says. "She is special."

Her cheeks color slightly at the compliment.

"Okay." I pick her up and back away. It's all I can do not to focus on the young, infinitely alluring woman in my arms. Every instinct makes me want to devour her, to taste her blood, to have her whole. To make her *mine*.

It's a struggle to push all those things aside.

"Ready?" I whisper.

She steadies herself against me. "Yes."

I take off at a run. I move as fast as my legs will carry me. The invisible ward is coming up in front of us. At the very last moment I spin back, crashing through it with my shoulders and clutching Eleira to me so she doesn't get crushed.

There's a tug, a resistance, and for an awful moment I think I'm going to lose her. Her body jerks as it hits the barrier. She cries out in pain from the force of impact. Momentum keeps us going forward, and my hands wrap more tightly around her so as not to let her go.

Time seems to slow as we traverse the barrier. I feel the force against her body, going the other way... and then there's a harsh *snap*, and both of us break through.

She rebounds into me. I stagger back, but I manage to stay on my feet.

"Are you okay?" I ask, concern filling every part of my soul.

She bobs her head up and down. She offers a weak smile. "We did it," she says.

"*You* did it," I correct. "This was my screw up, and you fixed it."

"Well, don't you worry your handsome face," she says. She sounds a little woozy. She brings a hand up and holds it to my cheek. "It's been fixed."

Her words tug at my heart. In particular, the part of my heart I didn't know existed.

Phillip appears next to us. "I hate to interrupt this tender moment," he says, "but we've got bigger issues to worry about."

He points. From out of the cavern opening stream dozens of Convicted. They're running straight at us.

They've sighted their prey.

I hand Eleira off to Phillip. "Go!" I tell them. "Get her up to the opening! I'll hold them off while you climb."

"There are too many, Raul!" Phillip cries. "You won't be able to stop them. Come with us!"

I grab him by the shoulder and shove him away. "Don't argue. Just go!"

The moans of The Convicted turn into vicious snarls. They'll attack as a pack.

Phillip looks at me, hesitating for a flicker of a moment. Then a crisp determination shows in his eyes. "Hang on tight," he tells Eleira, and, swinging her onto his back, he begins the scampering ascent to freedom.

I don't get to see how far they get, because at that moment, the horde falls on me.

Chapter Thirty-Eight

ELEIRA

Breaking through the ward was the single most impulsive, riskiest thing I have ever done.

I lied to the two vampire brothers. The spot I'd chosen was no weaker than any other. But in the face of what was coming, I didn't have any choice.

The truth of how I got through undoubtedly has to do with the transformation's progression. After my night vision came to me, I felt a new strength creep into my body. It wasn't over-whelming. In fact, it was very, very subtle.

The only reason I noticed it was that the injury I'd sustained when I was thrown off Phillip's back seemed to heal... faster. Or, at least, the after-effect of that was not as severe as I would have expected.

And now I'm back on Phillip's back, and he's scaling the cliff-face to our escape.

Sounds of a battle rage from below. I dare a glance down and see Raul throwing off one Convicted after the other. They all but ignore him, instead racing to get to me. The ones who engage with him are quickly destroyed.

"Faster, Phillip, faster!" I urge. He's not as adept at climbing as his brother. We're only a third of the way up. The Convicted start scaling the wall below. They'll be on us quickly.

Philip grabs a handhold and leaps up. We fly through the air. For a dizzying moment I feel weightless, and then he latches onto the next ledge.

"That fast enough for you?" he murmurs. "How's Raul doing?"

"They're not attacking him," I say. "They're focused on us!"

"Lucky they don't know the meaning of cooperation," he says. He jumps again, and catches a jagged piece of rock. The Convicted are swarming like beetles below us. They scurry up with a single-minded determination. A female in a red jacket loses her grip when one of her companions grabs her leg and tugs it to help himself. She falls, screaming.

I turn my head away before I can see the impact she makes on the ground.

Phillip finds a series of sure grips and quickly moves along them. We're closing in on the opening. Hope blossoms inside me—

I hear a wretched scream below. I look down. Raul is surrounded by four or five Convicted. They've finally turned their attention to him. He has deep gashes on his back and arms and legs and is bleeding badly.

"No!" I cry out.

One of The Convicted takes a swipe at him. Claws flash. Raul does not react in time to parry the attack. He screams again as the claws sink into his shoulder.

"We have to help him!" I cry out.

"No. You're more important. We need to get you to safety first." Phillip leaps up again. My heart flies to my throat. "There's the prophecy to consider and all that," he adds under his breath.

"But they're going to kill him!"

"Not if I know my brother." The sounds of the climbing hoard make urgency pulse through my body.

"You can't see what's going on!" I protest.

"We're almost there, Eleira." Phillip grunts and scampers up another dozen feet. "I'll help him once you're safe."

Chapter Thirty-Nine

RAUL

One of The Convicted wraps his arms around my neck in a stranglehold. I scream in rage and fling him off. His body crashes into the midst of those surrounding me, knocking them off their feet.

I spin around, tense and ready for the next attack. I'm surrounded by the mass. Anything I do, anything I try, is a losing prospect.

My eyes flicker up. I see Phillip scampering up the wall. Eleira is clinging to his back.

There's already a wave of Convicted climbing after them.

Another one tries to attack. I dodge the blow and land a fist in his middle. He doubles over from the strike, but he's already forgotten.

I need to give Phillip and Eleira more time.

My mind races for a solution as I zone out and fight on instinct alone.

Most of The Convicted rush past me, following the scent of blood.

A spark of an idea comes to mind. It's risky, and uncertain, but...

I grab The Convicted closest to me — it's a woman vampire. Or at the least, it used to be. Now she's little more than a walking corpse.

I bare my fangs and sink my teeth into her neck. Her horrid, tainted blood flows into me. It's no better than poison, but I need to have it, for what I'm about to do next.

I discard her body once she's drained dry. That happens in a matter of seconds. My own system recoils from the tainted blood. But I must have more, as much of it as I can stand without fainting.

I grab my next victim. This one was a man. My fangs go into the artery by his throat. His blood is even more corrupt, even more sickening. He's has been trapped here in the depths for much longer. Tasting his blood is like tasting death. Instead of the life-giving, energizing nectar that human blood is, this is a vile mix of liquefied maggot and ash.

I release the man. His body falls. *One more.* I need one more.

I grab the nearest Convicted. But shock paralyzes me for a moment when I see his face. I know this vampire—or at least, I used to. Ten years ago he'd been my Mother's lover. Then he disappeared without a trace. The story was he went rogue and left the safety of our coven to strike out on his own.

My surprise leaves me vulnerable. The split-second is enough for my opponent to strike at me.

He's stronger than the other Convicted. He's only been here a decade. The deprivation has not yet affected him as it has the rest.

His claws rip into my torso. I scream at the sudden influx of pain. The blood of the other Convicted that is in my body shatters all the defenses I have against such pain.

My blood-curdling yell attracts the attention of those nearby. Before I know it I'm surrounded by four of the Convicted who all have their focus on me. One attacks me from behind. I sense it, and I can move out of the way to dodge the strike, but I don't.

Claws sharp as a rake rip over my back. The tainted blood inside me bursts out.

Another one swipes at my legs. I jump back and shift my

body—but not to avoid him.

I do it to make sure the attack connects.

This is my maniacal, borderline suicidal plan.

In seconds, I'm covered in my own blood. The pain is horrible, but the scent... the scent, the smell, is overwhelming. It's made all the more potent by the dirtied blood flowing through me.

It reaches The Convicted climbing after Eleira and Phillip. It stops them in their tracks. For a moment, it confuses them.

And then, all their attention shifts to me.

I feel a momentary sense of triumph as the ones closest to my brother and the girl turn away and start climbing down. Human blood is sweet to them, yes, but the raw *strength* of mine, after it's been amplified by my two feedings, is the stronger bait.

And then the entire horde closes in on me, and my world goes black.

Chapter Forty

ELEIRA

My breath catches as the gap to The Convicted below us lessens. Phillip is climbing as fast as he can, but he's carrying an extra weight. And the monsters are driven by the scent of blood.

Suddenly, the opening appears before us. Light from the starry night sky outside filters in.

Phillip shoves me through. "Go!" he says. "Go now. I'll —"

He doesn't get to finish. One of The Convicted grabs his ankle and jerks him off his feet.

"No, Phillip!" I cry out. I grab for him, but he disappears over the edge. The snarling beasts are so close that I know I only have seconds. Even if they can't see the opening, common sense tells me they'll be able to find it by following the scent of my blood.

And I don't know if the ward is a physical barrier or merely an illusion for them.

I feel like such a coward, and I hate myself for it, but there's nothing I can do to help the brothers who rescued me.

So I turn, and, biting down a cry, lurch into an awkward run to get away.

Chapter Forty-One

PHILLIP

As soon as I get Eleira through the opening I stop and look down.

I know what my brother has done. He's sacrificed himself to give her a chance. I couldn't let her know that's the only reason she got out unscathed.

There's a dogpile of The Convicted right below me. More are streaming in from the sides. My gut clenches. Raul is underneath.

Please don't let me be too late, I pray.

A hand tugs on my foot. That's all the incitation I need. I turn, push off the ledge, and plunge straight down.

I land into the roiling mass of bodies. The fight has become an absolute melee. Convicted are fighting with Convicted. There's blood everywhere, they're tearing each other to pieces, to shreds.

I battle through the bodies looking for my brother. "Raul!" I scream. "Rau! Raul!"

A Convicted attacks me. For the first time in centuries, I release the precise hold I have over my vampire instincts... and fight back.

He rips at me, and I parry him and hit him back. My clawed hand connects with his face. Red lines of blood erupt around his deathly-pale skin. One more swipe, and my other hand separates his head from his body.

Exhilaration takes me. I feel... alive. I'm alive as I've never been before. I'm strengthened by an overwhelming sense of pride, and purpose: *I have to save Raul.*

Finally it's my turn to show my strength. It's my turn to prove my worth, my turn to demonstrate that I'm just as worthy of being a Prince as either of my brothers.

Another Convicted attacks me. I dance with him. From the corner of my eye I see a bloodied body lying limp on the floor.

It's Raul.

A savage hatred overtakes me. I've always been one for peace, but the nature of these creatures, attacking without mercy, without reason, repels me. I let go of my conscious mind and let my body do what it was designed to do:

Kill.

One after another of The Convicted falls at my hands. But there are too many. I try to get to my brother, but I cannot. For a second, I glimpse an opening — an escape. My path to safety.

Yet I will never abandon Raul.

So I turn away from the temptation. Raul and I are both going to die here. I know it. I know that this is where it all ends, where the tale of the two youngest Soren brothers comes to a close. James will inherit command. He'll marry Eleira and wrestle the throne from her hands, and all that we've done will have been for naught.

So be it. I'd rather die with my brother than be called a coward.

Suddenly, a great pillar of flame cuts a sweeping line just above my head.

I have no idea what's going on. I drop down. The Convicted scream and scatter once they feel the heat. They fear fire even more than regular vampires do. In their state, they are creatures with only the most primitive minds. Their instincts are amplified, so their fear is made ever greater.

The line of fire sweeps overhead again. It's close enough to burn some of the taller ones, or the ones unfortunate enough to have been thrown up in the brawl. The horrid reek of burning flesh mingles with their pained screeches.

I press myself closer to the ground and crawl toward my brother. I feel the heat of the sweeping flame. I don't have time to think of or consider its source. All I know is that I have to get to Raul.

After a few seconds, I reach him. My hand falls upon his wrist. I search desperately for a pulse. All my concentration goes to that last bit of hope, the tiny flutter that might tell me my brother is still alive.

There! I feel it. It's faint, and oh, so weak, but he's hanging on.

Barely.

The screams of The Convicted continue as they flee. They're getting farther and farther away.

I chance a look up, in the direction of the fire's source.

And there, at the mouth of the nearest cave, I find my Mother, wielding a long walking staff made of polished emerald. Flames gush out from its end, chasing The Convicted away.

She looks absolutely furious.

She spins the staff in her hands, and a fiery vortex breaks out in the shape of a cyclone. She sends it toward the last of The Convicted. She summons another one, and sends a second wave. Again and again she calls forth the destructive, fiery tornados and uses them to clear a space for the three of us.

When the last of The Convicted is gone… Mother's knees buckle. She catches herself on the staff.

I jerk up in alarm, but I don't go toward her. I'm afraid if I release Raul, it will be his end.

"Feed him, you fool!" she screams from across the cavern floor.

Of course! I cut an incision in my wrist with my fangs and press it to Raul's mouth.

"Come on, come on, come on," I mutter.

He's not drinking. My blood is flowing down my hand and simply dribbling over his chin.

"DRINK, DAMN YOU!" I scream. "DRINK!"

Raul gives a feeble cough. His lips part just enough to let my blood in. A drop, at first, then another, and one more…

Mother hobbles toward us. I've never seen her as anything

less than perfectly in control and perfectly strong. Now, her weakness is on full display. I don't know how her magic works, but the spells she cast have obviously taken their toll.

"Come on, Raul. Come on," I say. He is still not drinking fast enough. His heartbeat is frighteningly feeble. The pulse is no stronger than the distant ticking of a clock.

Mother reaches us. "What are you doing?" she exclaims. She sees Raul's mangled form. "Oh Lord, what's been done?"

"He won't drink!" I say.

"He must! Oh, Raul, Raul, Raul..."

She throws herself at him and sobs against his chest. "Don't leave me, no, don't leave us, please don't go!"

I've never seen her so distraught. Her body shakes with her despairing cries.

Determination grips me. Raul *must* drink. I force my wrist into his mouth and open his jaw so that every bit of my blood gets taken in.

He coughs again. Then his body jerks, and he twists to the side to spit all that I've given him out.

"What's happening?" I gasp.

"He's rejecting your blood," she says.

"Then give him yours!"

Mother gasps. "I would," she says, sounding scandalized. "Oh, trust me, Phillip, I would. But it would weaken me so, and I don't have enough, not after that exertion. We would both die."

I stare at her, awash in disbelief. She wouldn't do it for her *son?*

She begins to cry again.

But then realization hits, and my mind connects the dots.

"Get *away* from him!" I scream. I pick Raul up and rush him to the far wall. The look I saw in her eyes when she denied her son her blood... it was like that of a jilted lover.

And I understand: *She was using her magic to make Raul spit out my blood.*

As soon as we're away I press my bleeding wrist back to his lips. To my immense relief, Raul begins to suckle on the flow. Morgan stares at us both with undisguised hatred. But it lasts only the moment necessary for my blood to infuse with Raul's and bring him back to consciousness.

He opens his eyes. And Mother surges up, and exclaims, "It's a miracle!"

I shield my older brother from her with my body. I keep my wrist at his mouth. "Drink," I tell him. "As much as you need, you drink."

While Raul recovers, I keep a wary eye on our Mother.

She smiles at me like a cat.

"Enough," Raul finally says, pushing my arm away. His voice shakes, and he hangs onto me for support, but I know his stubborn pride won't let him take in more. "Where is Eleira?" he begins. "Where is —"

He cuts off when his eyes land on our Mother.

"What's *she* doing here?" he hisses.

"She," Morgan pronounces grandly, "saved both your sorry hides. *She* is the reason you two are still alive."

She gives a little laugh. "You are lucky I had the foresight to extend the ward underground."

Raul jerks to me. "She *knows*?"

"Of course I know," she says. "Did you think I could really let our future Princess out of my sight without *marking* her? Oh, I have a heart, I gave her some semblance of privacy. But the moment her body came in contact with my ward, I knew *exactly* where she was."

She begins a slow, calculated walk toward us. "You see, my sweet," she addresses Raul, "I would never enter Eleira in The Hunt. Not truly. What happened at the draft was nothing more than a way for me to see where *your* loyalty lies." She wipes at a non-existent tear. "How it breaks my heart that it is not with your family."

I step forward, ready to defend my brother. "Raul is—"

"Oh Phillip, did you think I was talking to you? No, no. Now the two powerful vampires are speaking. Don't forget your rank."

The reproach stings. I know that *logically,* it shouldn't affect me. But that vampire hierarchy of deference to those stronger than you is an instinct ground deeper than all the rest.

"Phillip has equal right to speak as I do," Raul says.

Mother smiles sadly. "Always the dreamer, you are."

"So what now?" Raul says. "You played your little trick. You've had your fun. But guess what? Eleira still got away."

Mother laughs. "You think you've freed her? Raul, how you disappoint me. Truly, you do. You know who she is, and you know how much of a draw she will be to the vampire who first drew her blood."

"James," Raul and I say in the same breath.

"Yes. James. And you just let the human girl out into the world, outside of my protection. Who do you think will come for her? Who do you think will be drawn back when he senses her emergence into the unprotected sphere?" She smiles sweetly. "You are a fool, Raul. A good-hearted man, perhaps, but a fool nonetheless. You are an *idealist.*"

He pushes off from me. "I have to go after her."

"Not so fast." Morgan waves her hand, and a silver chain bolts out from under her sleeve like a striking viper.

It catches Raul around the neck.

"What are you doing?" he cries out. He fights it, but silver is our weakness. It is the only material we cannot break.

"Why, sentencing you, of course. For treason against your Queen. For endangering the whole of our coven with your rash stupidity."

"But Eleira—"

"*Phillip* will go after her. Won't you, weakest?"

I flinch. She hasn't called me that since the earliest days of The Haven.

Raul turns to me. I can see the turmoil in his eyes. "Please," he says. "Please get her back."

"So sweet," Mother murmurs. "I'm touched. Really, I am." She motions to the opening above me in a shooing gesture. "Well, go on then, off you go. Nobody will miss you here."

I steel myself. "I'll find her," I promise Raul. "I—"

The word is cut off as Mother launches a second silver chain at me. It wraps around my throat like a snake. Pain erupts from the metal's touch.

"On the other hand…" she says. "Raul really *is* better suited for the outside world. I've changed my mind." She jerks me to her. I fall that way with the collar. It's sapping all my strength. I know it's not just ordinary silver. It has to be imbued with one of her awful spells.

"Raul," she announces. "You will go. But if you don't bring Eleira back before the next full moon," the chain tightens around my throat. "Your brother will die."

Chapter Forty-Two

ELEIRA

I break through into the cool night air on the other side of the tunnel. I strain my ears for any hint of pursuit.

I hear nothing. No screams, no sounds of battle, absolutely... nothing.

I didn't realize it when I was running, but apparently the ward that seals The Convicted also blocks all sound.

I collapse against a nearby tree. I try hard to catch my breath. I feel exhausted, and yet, at the same time, exhilarated and alive.

A few minutes pass. I feel a bit more stable. Then realization sinks in.

I've just escaped The Haven.

Holy crap! The magnitude of that staggers me. Did I really, for a few moments, actually consider going back and helping the two creatures who'd *captured* me? I mean, yes, they helped me out, but if it wasn't for them none of this ever would have happened. I wouldn't have *needed* to escape.

And yet that pang of guilt hits me again. Is this Stockholm Syndrome on display?

I push the thought from my mind. I've gotten out of The Haven. I never thought it possible, not truly, so I never thought of what I would do next.

I do know one thing, though. The longer I stay here, the worse my odds are of *really* getting away. Morgan might have already discovered my absence. She wouldn't hesitate to put on a full-out manhunt to find me.

I look up at the sky. I'm in luck that it's still night on this side of the ward. The stars give me something to navigate by.

I push off and head west. If I'm still in California—which I think I am, given the trees and temperature—west will bring me to the coast. That's where civilization will be.

The only question is… how long will it be until I find it?

Yet after just half an hour of walking, doubts fill my mind. I'm not human anymore. I'm in the process of becoming something else.

Can I really trust myself to make it on my own? I know so little about the creature I'm about to become. What if there are dangers to the transformation, things that only vampires can warn me about?

This is like puberty again, but with a capital P. Scratch that. It's puberty in all-caps with a trifecta of exclamation marks behind it.

Weariness hits me. I put a hand over my eyes and lean against the trunk of a tree. This is crazy. Isn't it? I got my heart's desire, which was to escape. But now that I'm here, the prospect is almost meaningless.

How can I return to my old life? It will be impossible. After everything that I've seen, the odds of me simply waltzing back to campus and settling into my old routine is ludicrous. I'll never be able to forget The Haven.

It's not just the place. It's the *people*, the humans living there, crushed by the vampires' rule.

What can I do from the Outside? Call the cops? I snort a laugh. I'd just as soon be put in a mental institution. Nobody I talk to will think me anything but crazy.

Then there's April. My reluctant friend stuck on the inside. I can't just abandon her. I can't just… run away from all this.

I bite hard on the inside of my lip. I look to the west. The real world is that way. But my loyalties… my loyalties lie in the opposite direction.

With a strangled cry, I break away from the tree. I go back the way I came. I can't abandon all that I've come to know. No matter how twisted and cynical and seemingly unreal. In my heart, I know it *is* real.

"Sorry, Mom. Sorry, Dad," I whisper. If I get the chance, I'll contact them. But not now. What would I say? *Your daughter's been selected as the heir to a vampire dynasty. Oh, and by the way, she's also likely not to survive past the next full moon?*

No. Better to leave them in the dark for now. Only once I figure my way, with Raul's and Phillip's help, will I be in a position to reach out to them.

I just hope I manage to reach that position first.

Chapter Forty-Three

ELEIRA

I can't find my way back.

I can't find my way back. I got twisted around when I tripped and fell over a root, and now all the trees look familiar, identical, and dark clouds cover the sky, and they block the moon and the stars, and I have no idea where I'm going, and I'm lost, and, and, and —

I cut off my thoughts before they can descend into deeper panic. I need to reunite with Raul and Phillip. They'll know what to do. They'll know where to go from here.

A branch snaps somewhere in the dark. My breath hitches as I spin toward it. My heart begins to pound.

I feel a... presence, looming in the darkness.

"Who's there?" I call. I try to keep my voice strong.

Nothing. No reply, no acknowledgment... nothing.

The only thing I hear is the rustle of the wind through the

redwoods.

But my vision allows me to see farther than before. I strain my eyes to pierce the black. And...

There!

Was that a flash of movement in the night? Was that a darkened shape darting over the forest floor?

My whole body tenses. I'm still very much in vampire territory. For all I know, it could be one of them, drawn forth by my blood.

Anxious seconds pass. And then...

A wolf emerges from the trees.

My breath catches. He's beautiful, with a full silver coat and sharp, gleaming eyes.

I stand entranced as he approaches. His eyes lock into mine... but I feel no fear. His steps are graceful and sleek. He's a male in the prime of life, and he's massive. He stands almost up to my chest. I feel power radiate from him. I feel his innate, inherent capacity for great violence. I should be terrified, but I'm not.

He walks right at me, and then, not five feet away, stops and sits on his haunches.

His cunning eyes pierce mine. I feel an instant familiarity with the animal. A kinship. There is no fear, only a wonderful sense of awe.

Am I crazy? Am I imagining things that are not there?

But if the wolf posed any danger to me, I would know it. Both of us remain very still, lost in the moment, admiring each other.

Then some kind of rodent runs through the bush, and the wolf spins and darts off. He's gone as fast as a silver bullet.

The trance is broken, and anxiety replaces my calm. I'm all alone again.

At least until I find my way back.

I start in a direction at random. Anything's better than standing still.

But I don't get more than ten feet when a hand clamps over my mouth. I give a muffled scream. Something sharp jabs into my neck.

"Not so fast, my darling," a dark, familiar voice whispers in my ear. I try to struggle but all my muscles are going lax.

The tranquilizer kicks in, and I lose consciousness.

***

I wake up with my arms and legs bound to a seat in a private plane.

Panic shoots through me. There's a gag in my mouth that prevents me from screaming. Not that I would try. The sight in front of me is more than enough to silence my tongue.

James.

He's wearing a dapper black suit, sitting casually with his legs crossed. He appears almost bored as his eyes glaze over me.

I jerk my wrists against the bonds. There's no give. I'm locked in tight.

"Silver." James points a casual finger at my restraints as he rolls his head side-to-side and yawns. "In the middle of the rope, you see. I wouldn't be so cruel as to let it touch your skin. That would prove very painful, for a half-vampire like you."

I glare at him. Is he in league with his two brothers? He *has* to be.

But if they helped me get out… why am I bound tight now?

"Oh, you look mad." He smiles. His drawl makes everything he says carry a sinister edge. "Don't be. I am very, very pleased with you."

He leans forward and smiles, placing both elbows on his thighs.

"You can't imagine how much easier you made things for me, darling. I would have thought it'd take me weeks, maybe months, to smuggle you out. But then as I got close, a scent caught my attention," he taps his nose. "And I *knew* you were Outside. However did you do it, I wonder? And with such fortuitous timing."

He gives a languid stretch. I continue to glare at him. Does he really not know why I was out of The Haven? Or is he just toying with me?

All my instincts point to the latter.

"Where's Raul?" I try to say. He betrayed me. I just know it. And to think, for a time I was starting to imagine having *feelings* for him.

"What's that?" He brings a hand to his ear. "You must be clearer. I really cannot understand you."

"Raul, Raul, Raul!" I say, the gag muffling all my words.

James spreads his hands. "I'm sorry, doll, but I just can't understand you." He shrugs. "Too bad."

"RAUL!" I all but scream.

"Here's an idea. What if I remove that horrible rag covering your mouth, and we can speak like civilized humans, hmm?" His eyes sparkle. "Or should I say, *vampires?*"

He reaches over and unties the rag. As soon as he does, I spit in his face.

He looks shocked. For a split-second he doesn't react.

Then anger flashes, distorting his handsome features, and he slaps me.

My head snaps to the side. I taste blood from my cheek. Before I know it, James has my chin in a vice-like grip. He forces my face to him.

"That," he growls dangerously, "was a very stupid move. You do something like that again," his eyes drop to my neck, "and you risk inciting my anger. You've been warned."

He lets go. His eyes continue to hone into me as he returns to his seat. He takes a white handkerchief out from one pocket and wipes the spit from his face.

"Now," he says, putting it away. "Can I trust you to be civil? I know it's a tall task for a teenage girl. But just… humor me and make the effort, will you?"

I keep my lips sealed and match his stare, one for one.

"Silence won't get you very far," he says. He gestures around the cabin. "Aren't you curious where we are? Where we're going?"

I say nothing.

He sighs. "I'll tell you, then. Right now, we're about halfway across the Pacific. We'll be making a short stop in Eastern Russia before continuing on our way."

"On our way where?" I ask grudgingly.

"Oh, but that's the surprise." He positively beams. "And you, my pure, sweet, soon-to-be-vampire, are the ultimate prize."

Chapter Forty-Four

RAUL

As soon as Mother drags Phillip away I scale the cliff and emerge Outside.

I wish I could say I couldn't believe she would hold her own son hostage, but I know her better than that. The six hundred years of her rule have been defined by such pockets of insanity. She's almost cost us the entire safety of The Haven with her capricious nature multiple times, particularly in the early years. Most recently, I thought she'd settled down, but it looks like I was wrong.

I would have gone after Phillip the moment she took him away if I had even the slightest chance of succeeding. But Morgan is the strongest vampire in the coven, and her strength is magnified by the magic she wields. Couple that with her silent, icy rage for having lost Eleira, along with my own sapped strength, and I wouldn't have stood a chance. She'd have destroyed us both, or worse, severed our souls and bound them into her perverse paintings.

So the only thing I could do was what she demanded of me. Like a coward, I had to leave my youngest brother.

"But I won't fail you, Phillip," I promise through gritted teeth. "Or you, Eleira."

I reach the end of the tunnel and come out amongst the trees. There's a breeze in the air that blows away from the secret entrance. I inhale deep, searching for Eleira's all-consuming scent.

And feel nothing.

I grunt in frustration. After all I've gone through, my body does not feel like my own. The fire, the fight with the guards, feeding the human woman my own blood then racing away at one fraction of my strength and taking on The Convicted, and then feeding on *their* horrible blood.

The only reason I'm standing is because of Phillip's infusion of his own blood. Even so, my system hasn't had time to clear the tainted blood. So everything I do now, everything I can do, is at one-tenth of my usual capacities, one-tenth, or worse.

I don't have time to rest, however. The land around The Haven is teeming with carnivorous creatures. Wild cougars and wolves and black bears stalk the woods.

That was one of my Mother's very first spells, cast at the foundation of The Haven. It lured all animal predators to us. Before she learned the secrets of the wards, our humans were penned inside by the knowledge that should they try to escape, they'd find merciless, hungry, rogue predators on the other side. Animals who would tear them limb from limb without a second's pause.

Over the centuries, the pull this land has on those types of creatures has only increased. So the forest is more dangerous than ever before.

That means Eleira has half an hour or less before she is scented as prey and attacked by one of the wild beasts.

I run forward, urging my body to heal faster. I need all the abilities I possess. But I feel blind as a bat in daylight. My senses are nowhere near as sharp as they should be. I cannot smell Eleira. I cannot hear her. I cannot feel her presence.

Then realization hits. I've been a vampire so long that I forgot — I have a voice.

So I cup my hands around my mouth and scream her name. "Eleira! Eleira! Eleira, where are you?"

I dash through the trees like a madman. My lurching movements are no better than a drunk's. The sky is starting to lighten overhead. Soon it'll be day, and I'll have to go underground to hide from the sun.

"Eleira!"

And then, the winds shift, and I catch the smell of blood. Hot blood, viscous blood, blood from something that was recently alive. Not Eleira's, but...

I run that way, breaking through overgrown branches, and stumble into a small, rocky clearing.

I go still.

The ruined body of a monstrous wolf lies among the rocks. Its silver fur is matted with red. There are slash marks on its back and neck and underbelly. Its front legs have been horribly broken.

But it's still breathing. It's alive.

"What is this?" I breathe.

I rush to it. The animal's pulse is weak. My brow creases with disquietude.

"Who would do this to you?" I say.

Then I catch the faintest whiff of somebody else's blood.

I recognize it immediately. It's my brother's.

James was here.

I give a savage roar. Only James would delight in torture like this. I hate that the animal has suffered for so long. Quickly, I grip the wolf's head and give one final, sharp twist to put it out of its misery.

But why was James here? Why was he back? Why and how? His diplomatic mission should have taken *weeks* —

An awful understanding washes over me. If James was here, and Eleira was Outside, alone and unprotected…

He would have gotten to her.

The weight of my failure crashes into me. Of course, I can't sense Eleira. She's no longer here.

Rage boils up inside. James can't have taken her to The Haven, or I would have run into them. Then where?

I don't know. But as I rise, a new determination grips me. One that washes away the anguish and the fear.

I vow, then and there, that I *will* find Eleira. I will go to the ends of the world to get her back. Because my brother has taken something from me that isn't his. Because no matter who bit her first, the girl *is* mine.

I feel the possessiveness in the deepest part of my soul. I haven't felt it since Liana, never thought I would feel it again. But with Eleira gone, and worse, with Eleira threatened…

Well, that part of me has awakened again.

Chapter Forty-Five

JAMES

I don't know what stroke of luck brought Eleira to me. But when the gods grant a boon, you do not snuff your nose at it.

I snort a laugh. *Gods*. There are no gods, only children of the night, only creatures of pure blackness, only...

Us.

I walk into the cockpit and take control of the plane. There's a special UV filter on the glass that protects me from the worst of the sun. It's nowhere near one-hundred percent — nothing can fully protect us from those painful rays except a complete barrier — but it's the only thing that makes flying like this bearable.

Of course, I could simply hire a pilot, but I always like doing things myself.

When Mother sent me away to negotiate with Father's coven — and to *kill* him — I thought her insane.

But I also saw it as an opportunity for me. Peace between the covens might be impossible — but peace was never what I had in mind.

Power was.

I walk for miles past the outskirts of the abandoned city, not once daring to use my speed.

I know I'm being watched. I feel it in my bones. My father's coven is ruled strictly and governed with military zest. Precision and security is of the utmost importance to him. Nothing happens within a hundred leagues of his home without his knowing.

I force my gait to be casual. I want to appear at ease.

Even if I'm going into the one place in the world no vampire has ever emerged from after entering.

In the distance, across the sands, I spot two lone figures. They stand and watch me.

Sentries. Sent out as my welcome.

One is a vampire almost as old as I am. The other...

A wave of shock washes through me when I feel the other's power. He's more than just old. He is ancient. Older than any vampire I have ever come across, or known could exist. Even from this far I can feel his strength, radiating out toward me like a warning beacon, telling me not to approach.

I force a crooked smile and pick my pace up just a little. One vampire who is my match, another who is many times stronger. Back in The Haven, all others of our coven would tremble in fear before such a foe.

And these are just the two spared to greet me.

I keep walking until I'm within arm's reach of them. The ancient one nods. I grin at him.

Suddenly, an invisible force strikes me in the chest. I'm sent sprawling. I come to a stop in the sand and look up.

The ancient one mimics my grin.

He used the Mind Gift against me! I marvel. It's a telekinetic force that only develops in the strongest of our kind. All I can do with it is roll a marble around on a table, or flip the page of a book, or maybe make a paperclip levitate for the briefest moment.

And he used it to knock me down.

I've never been one to bend the knee. But for this vampire, I have no choice. I bow my head in the ageless symbol of respect.

Before I know what's happening, the two vampires grab my

arms and cuff me. I don't fight. For one, because I wouldn't stand a chance. Two, because I'm not here as a threat.

The silver bracelets burn into my wrists. I grit my teeth and ignore the sensation. It's ridiculous how something so brittle can restrain creatures as powerful as we are.

I'm pulled to my feet roughly. I have half a mind to tell them who I am, but I'm sure they already know. Announcing my lineage will only make me seem weak.

"This way," the younger of the two says. "Your father is waiting."

Just as I thought.

We walk a distance into seemingly vacant sands. But at a certain point, we cross a threshold. The air shimmers, and the ancient ruins of a forgotten city are revealed.

The architecture is a strange mix of Roman and Arabic styles. There are half-collapsed columns next to beautiful monasteries and temples. Everything is made of a material the color of sand—I don't know what it's called, I've never been one to study such things.

I'm led down a twisting path through the city. There's not a single soul around us. Some of the structure have been completely restored, while others lie in crumbled ruins. There's no sense of guidance to it that I can decipher.

We reach a temple entrance. Wide stairs lead into the earth. I take one look up at the night sky and mutter a prayer hoping I'll see it again.

"Here." The younger vampire shoves something at me. I look.

It's a sack. The outside is inlaid with fine threads of silver, while the inside is covered in soft velvet.

The elder takes it by the silver side. It doesn't appear to inflict him any pain. "For your eyes and ears," he says, and slips it over my head.

Immediately, I'm cut off from all perception. The silver blocks my hearing, my vision, even my sense of direction. Strong arms take me from behind and guide me down the steps.

I cannot tell how long we journey for. The velvet layer on the inside saves me from the pain, but the silver on the outside inflicts a sensation like the most terrible headache. My thoughts become slow and sluggish. I can hardly distinguish who I am.

An indeterminable amount of time later, my blindfold is cast off.

I gape. I'm in the middle of an enormous circle of snarling, hissing, malevolent vampires.

My mind grapples with how many there are. Thousands. *Two thousand, three thousand — maybe more.*

And their strength. It's astounding! It pulses into me from all sides like with the irrepressible force of an ocean tide. I don't sense a single vampire in their midst weaker than I am.

For the first time in centuries, I feel a very real frisson of fear.

A door opens and slams shut. At the sound, all the vampires fall silent.

Heavy, plodding footsteps come from the distance. The King approaches.

Moments later, a passage opens in the bodies. Through the gap I see my father.

Instantly, I drop to both knees and kiss the ground.

It's a supplicating gesture, but I have no choice. My father's strength is two times that of the ancient one I'd met outside.

How? *I wonder. My mind works furiously to come up with an answer.* How could they all be so strong?

I wait there, trembling, for him to come. I hold literally no power here. I have absolutely no sway. Blood ties will only bring me so far, as they fade to insignificance in the face of raw strength.

I feel two heavy hands grasp me by the shoulder. "Rise, son," my father says. "Rise, and witness the beauty of my rule!"

I look up and catch his eyes. Then I gasp and avert my gaze. He has more than the telltale vampire ring of black around his irises. He has these black, floating specks that swim across the whites of his eyes. They look like signs of corruption—of him giving completely into the darkness.

But I don't know. I don't know, and it throws me off and ruins my confidence. I thrive on power, on the knowledge that I am the best. Here, I am nothing.

I have not felt like nothing since before my transformation began.

He pulls me to him and embraces me. A low, monosyllabic chanting starts around us.

Father lets me go. "It is good to see you after all these years."

"Likewise, Father." I muster. The chanting grows louder. It unnerves me.

"Are you impressed?" he asks. He gestures around him. The old chains and rings and bracelets that cover his hands and forearms and wrists clink together as he does. "These vampires are all loyal to me. All but one is younger than you."

I only just manage to stop my jaw from dropping.

"You have met that one already," Logan says. "It is his knowledge, coupled with my strength, that gives The Crypts its power."

"It is... wondrous," I say.

My father stands a fraction of an inch taller. He's just as vain as I am. "Yes," he agrees. "It is."

He cuts a hand sharply through the air. The chanting stops. Silence fills the room, but it's not a silence of the regular sort. Past it, in the background, is a reverberating hum that seems to come from the walls themselves.

"Witness my son's entry into The Crypts!" my father exclaims. "Am I not merciful to grant him passage? Am I not just to give him the fairness of a trial?"

A cheer erupts from the vampires surrounding us.

My father holds his arms up and does a slow turn to take the applause in. Then he sweeps them down, and another hush falls.

"I have made my decision," he says. He takes me by the shoulder. His grip holds me firmly in place. Even if I wanted to, I could never escape. "It is by your leave that I have made it. James will live. No vampire blood shall be spilled today. I offer him full guest rights in our home."

Another cheer erupts. Gooseflesh prickles my skin.

"He will be treated with all the courtesy extended to any of you. What's more —what's more! I hereby grant him leave to freely enter and exit The Crypts. No vampire has been given that in two hundred years! It is a gift worth the entire world!"

One more raucous cheer swells up. It's all I can do to take it in.

"Yes, yes," my father says, satiating in the adoration. "You are all my children, but he is my son!" He grasps my hand and thrusts it up. "He could be your Prince, if only..." my father's grip tightens on my palm. I suck in a pained breath. Any more pressure and he'd break all the small bones of my hand.

"...If only he did not come here to kill me!"

With a snarl he throws me to the ground. I land hard. The crowd hisses angrily. Before I can react, my father is on me, pinning me to the stone floor like a bug.

"What say you?" he demands of his subjects. He takes out a

*long, studded dagger and aims it at my heart. "After I have shown
him such mercy, after I have been so valiant and fair... he betrays
me so!"*

*The dagger flashes downward. My hands catch his wrist but
I'm weak as a toddler against his unbound strength. I can do nothing to protect myself.*

*The tip stops against my shirt. My father applies the faintest
bit of pressure. It spears through my jacket and presses into my
skin.*

*"Do I do it?" His head swings wildly around him, the black
flecks littering his eyes. "Do I kill my own son, because of what we
know? Because of what he came here to do?"*

"Father, no," I say. "I was sent, yes, but —"

*He backhands me. He does it with the most casual of gestures,
but it makes my neck snap violently to the side.*

"I did not ask you," he growls.

*I bite down an angry retort and meet his murderous glare. "Do
it, then," I hiss.*

"Mercy!" somebody cries out.

My father jerks his attention toward the voice. "A call for mer-

cy?" he asks. "Who gives it? Step forth!"

Out from the milling bodies steps a beautiful blonde woman. Her skin is tanned. Tanned skin. On a vampire!

I've never seen the like.

That's not all. Her eyes are green and soft. Yet there's an edge to them that I'm immediately drawn to, a challenge that says she's not one to back down.

"State your case," my Father says.

"Show him mercy, my King." She goes to one knee and plants a fist in the ground. "If you spare him, I will bear responsibility for his actions."

A dozen malicious sneers come from the vampires closest to her. She ignores them all.

"You would risk you own position in our sanctuary for a vampire you do not know?"

"I know he is your son," she says. "And I know how great a leader you have been to us."

My father's dagger eases off. A tad. "Go on."

"It would be a waste to kill him, my King. Lend him to me. I will take him under my protection. He has," she licks her lips, "po-

tential."

"Hmm." My father looks around. "Do any others feel the same way? Does anyone else stand for my son?"

The silence that comes is deafening.

Logan looks to me — and leaps off. He offers me his hand. I grudgingly accept. He pulls me to my feet.

"Very well," he says. "All the gifts I bestowed upon you with guest rights still stand. When in The Crypts, you will be under Victoria's care. See that you represent her well." He strikes his hands together. "The ceremony is done! You may now return to your lives."

The vampires scatter, leaving only me, my Father, and Victoria standing there.

***

"Why did you speak for me?"

I'm pacing the empty floor in the middle of my guest chamber. Victoria brought me here, sat on a stool, and has been silent ever since.

I repeat my question. She simply watches me like an odd curiosity.

My anger rises. But I cannot display it here, for even she is *stronger than I. And she can't have been made more than a hundred years ago!*

Whatever the secret is to their strength, I need it. I need it more than I need air and passion. I need it more than I need blood.

I turn on her. "Answer me!"

She taps her lips.

"Why won't you speak? You had no trouble with it in front of the King!"

"I find," she says finally, "that the more I let men talk, the more information they will give out for free."

She grins and hops down from her spot. She's a lot shorter than she seemed to be when I first saw her from the floor.

I grunt. "And what information have I given you?"

"That you're rash. Impetuous." She waltzes up to me and runs a finger along my chest. "All qualities," she says, looking into my eyes, "that I like most in a man."

I stare at her. "Is that what this is?" I say softly. "A seduction?"

"Hardly," she laughs. She pushes me away and spins around. "I simply thought you might be useful to have on my side."

"So you pick at the bottom of the barrel to find an ally." I can't hide the disdain in my voice. I am used to being strong, but in The Crypts, I am no better than a fledgling.

"Oh, you give yourself too little credit, James." She twirls a strand of her pretty hair. "You have the King's blood in you. You could be Prince."

I scoff. "If it wasn't for you, my Father would have killed me. Tell me, what type of Prince am I?"

"One who hasn't glimpsed his full potential," she replies. "One who doesn't know the things he is capable of."

"I don't lack confidence in my abilities... when I know what I'm up against. Here?" I gesture angrily around the walls. "Everybody here is stronger. How can that be?"

Her eyes twinkle as she regards me and considers the question. "You've been around a long time," she says. "What do you think?"

"If I knew, I wouldn't be asking!" I explode.

That laugh comes again. It reminds me of Mother's.

"Who are you, Victoria?" I ask. "What do you really want with me?"

"I want," she lounges on the bed. "The same thing that you do. Power. *I see how you crave it. I see it in your eyes.*"

I sneer. "Power? You have it. You're stronger than I—"

"Not strength." *She clicks her tongue in irritation.* "Strength is easy. Everybody here is granted strength."

"I don't understand."

"You think a vampire's abilities are static? You think once one is transformed, a vampire stays the same?"

"Of course not. We grow stronger as we age and feed. Don't lecture me. I've been on this earth five times as long as you."

"Or more," she says casually.

"More?" My voice is flat.

"I was made forty years ago."

I simply stare. She has forty years, compared to my six-hundred? That's all the time it's taken her to surpass me in strength?

"Strength is an illusion, James. Strength comes and goes. It can increase, just as it can fade. But power... power lasts forever."

"Forgive me," I say sourly, "If I don't see the distinction."

"You *have* power," she says. She points to me. "You may not know it, but it's there, lying latent in you, like a great beast waiting to be awakened. It comes from your bloodline. I —" she flips her hair back, "— possess only strength. What you see, with me, is what you get."

And it's a damn lot more than me, *I think.*

"I can tell you the secret," she says sweetly. "'I know it's eating away at you. 'How can a vampire so much younger be so much stronger?' The question is clear on your face."

"Our powers grows as we age and drink blood," I repeat. "There's no way to expedite the process."

She smiles. "And yet here you are. And here I am. And the contrast between our abilities is simply... staggering."

My jaw tightens. "How, then?" I say.

"The Blood of the Ancient."

I advance on her. "Tell me."

"You met him. You felt him. You know his strength."

"Yes," I say. "But he would not spread his blood amongst all of this coven. What vampire would share? There are too many here, he would be a shell. No," I shake my head. "He could not have given it away. Not like that."

"Are you truly so limited in your beliefs," she asks, "that you think there is only one way of transferring strength?"

My head snaps to her. "What do you mean?"

"There is a chalice," she explains, "rimmed with eighteen rubies. It's an ancient artifact, guarded jealously by your father. It is what lets him rule."

"How do you know this?" I ask.

"There's little of The Crypts I don't know," she answers obscurely.

"Who are you?" I ask her again.

"Someone with ambition," she tells me. "Someone... a lot like you."

"Fine." She won't give me a better answer, and I'm in no position to press. "So this chalice. What does it do?"

"One drop of the Ancient's blood, placed inside the rim, multiplies and expands to be enough to feed our whole coven," she says. "The rubies on the edge are infused with a dark and powerful magic. There are ceremonies held, every ninety days, in which that blood is shared with all. But," she sighs, "only the tiniest portion is given to us. Your father hordes the majority of it for himself."

My eyes fill with greed. "The chalice is key to his power," I say.

"Yes," she nods slowly. "Now you're starting to understand. His rule is accomplished by two things. On the one hand is the Ancient's unwavering loyalty to him. On the other, is —"

"The magic chalice," I say. My excitement is growing. "What more do you know of it? Does it enhance anybody's blood? What if a vampire drinks more than is distributed by the ceremony?"

"Well then, such a vampire becomes even stronger," she says. She comes to me. "The potential of such a vampire becomes… limitless."

My mind swims with the possibilities. "If I controlled the chalice…"

"We," she corrects.

I nod impatiently, "If we were to control it…"

"Then we would rival any who walk this earth," she says.

I start pacing briskly about the room. My strides are long and sharp to go along with my thoughts. "The strength the chalice gives, it's temporary?" I ask. "That is why the ceremonies take place

again and again. Am I right? Or does every drink build on the previous one?"

"Temporary," she agrees. "You want to know why none who enter The Crypts ever leave? Why they all have such loyalty to the
King? It's because he has them all addicted. Who would turn
away?"

"But you're different," I say. "Why? What's made you so?"

Her eyes take on a shadowy look. "This and that," she says softly.

"This and that," I repeat flatly.

"Yes," she snaps. "This and that."

I stop in front of her. She stares up at me, defiance clear in her
eyes.

I want to kiss her.

I don't, of course. The natural hierarchy of power stands in the
way of that. But if I had a sip from the chalice, if I could have even
the briefest understanding of that strength. . .

"You don't share the others' loyalty."

"No."

"You would go against your King."

"Yes."

"Why?"

"I have my reasons. Will you help?"

"You knew," I pledge, going down to one knee, *"that I would be yours from the moment you saved me."*

Until it's my turn to rise above.

Chapter Forty-Six

JAMES

Victoria takes me on a brief tour of The Crypts. There are many places she is not allowed. The boundaries only increase with me as a companion.

So after a fruitless hour we return to my room. "I still don't understand." I tell her, "Why you are taking a chance on me."

"Maybe it's you who is taking a chance on me," she replies. "I could be leading you to your destruction."

"You saved me from that."

"And how long will your loyalty last, I wonder? Until you get what you want? What is it that you want, James?"

"How did my father know I was sent here to kill him?"

Her eyebrows rise. "You admit to that?"

"He proclaimed it as fact."

"That is why I chose you."

"Yes, but how did he know?"

She considers. "When you came upon us," she says. "Above ground. Did the Ancient greet you?"

"Yes."

"Did you let him touch you?"

I think back. "Yes."

"That is how he knew. The Ancient has powers greater than you imagine. When he made contact, he saw the truth of your heart."

"But I did not intend to kill my father. Not truly. I was sent for that, yes, but —"

"And that is why he let you live!" she laughs. "Did you think I could really influence him? All I did was provide a nudge in the other direction. It was all his choice."

"And now he knows I am bound to you."

"And me to you."

"You're different from the others," I say. "Aren't you?"

"You know I am."

"You did not want to be like this." I gesture at us. "You did not

want to be a vampire. You resent what you have become."

She considers, then shakes her head. "No. I resent the way I was made. I am grateful for what I have become."

"You want to stand on your own. Don't you? You crave autonomy."

"Wouldn't you?" she asks me heatedly. "If you spent your whole life being raised like a pig for slaughter, wouldn't you resent those who had done it to you?"

Something finally clicks in my head. "You come from one of the five witch clans! Don't you? That's the only reason you are the way you are!"

"Independent?"

"No. Defiant."

She sighs. "When I was born," she says, "an evil creature came in the night and murdered my family. My mother, my father, my brother and sister—none were left alive... save for me. I was made an orphan and abandoned in the world.

"When I was ten that same creature found me again. He was a young man and strikingly beautiful. He slipped through my window in the middle of the night and offered me a choice; come with him,

or end up like the rest of my family. He said he was there to finish the job.

"I screamed. The nuns heard. Before they could rush to my room the young man swept me up in his arms and whisked me away. I was brought," she grimaces, "here. Into The Crypts. Destined to never again see the sun."

"But your skin," I say. "It's golden. How?"

"That deprivation made me yearn for the sunlight more than anything else. When I was turned and had my freedom given back to me—I went out into the day."

"That should have killed you," I breathe.

"It nearly did. The Ancient found me and gave me his blood. Not from the chalice. From himself."

I suck in a breath of surprise.

"Something broke inside of me then. A shift, and ever since, I was different from the rest. I survived and know the sun cannot kill me. The pain when I go out, of course, is nearly unbearable, but I have that which no other vampires possess."

"Freedom," I say.

"Of a sort. But there was only one reason The Ancient rescued

me that day. It was the same reason the young vampire killed my family and left me alive."

"Your ancestral bloodline," I say. "Going back to the clans."

She nods. "I've studied the celestial charts. I know who I am." She flexes a fist. "And," she adds in a softer tone, "whom I was mistaken to be."

"What do you mean?"

"It was my sister, my twin, who your Father needed. She was the one born at the proper time, when the zodiacs were in position to grant her the gift of magic. But the one who was sent after me made a mistake and killed her, while letting me live.

"He was punished for it, of course, when the truth came out. But it was after I was turned. Only then did they realize I was not her. That I was of no use to your father as a proper witch."

"Yet you're still alive."

She gives a coy smile. "I have other talents that men find useful."

A spark of attraction flares inside me.

"The others here hate me for it. I was your father's mistress for a number of years." She sighs. "Until he grew bored of me. But it *was enough to guarantee my life."*

"And now you're on your own." I'm starting to understand Victoria a lot more. "You're on your own, and you need an ally. Somebody with no ties to others in The Crypts."

"Except for the strongest tie of all," she says. "Believe me, James. We will exploit that tie, and I will have vengeance on those who killed my family. With the chalice in our hands, you and I will be unstoppable."

"But how do we get it?" I ask. "I don't know the layout of this place. I am blind to the currents of power."

"You are the king's son," she says. "And I am his former lover. We will find a way. But first..." Her eyes glimmer. "We need us a proper witch."

Chapter Forty-Seven

ELEIRA

The plane makes a rough landing, and James emerges from the pilot's cabin.

I glare at him. "Where are we? What do you want with me?"

He leans back and crosses his arms. "Your cooperation," he says.

"Like I would ever help you."

"You think you have a choice?" He leaps at me, crossing the space in a single bound. He pins me to the back of the seat. "You think you have any *say* in what happens to you?"

He wants me to be scared. In truth, I feel terrified, but I would never let him know.

I meet his eyes and lift my chin. "You're not going to kill me," I declare. "If you were, I'd already be dead."

He laughs. "Is that your greatest concern?"

He grabs my hair by the roots and jerks my head to one side.

A long expanse of my neck is exposed. I feel extra-vulnerable.

He brings his lips to my ear. "Eleira," he whispers. "You must know there are fates worse than death."

He circles the spot where he once bit me with his fingers.

"Once," he continues, "not so very long ago, I would have given anything to have you in my grasp. To have you alone, with me, like this, so that I could do absolutely anything I wanted…" he tightens his fist in my hair, and I flinch in pain, "…to you."

He lets go and steps away. "But situations *change*. Circumstances change. Destinies and needs and wants, all shift and shimmer, like leaves dancing in the wind."

"How poetic," I deadpan.

He flashes an evil smile. "It's not my intention to impress you with poetry. All I need to do is keep you alive until the transformation truly begins."

"Where are we?" I repeat.

"A safe place. You could say… we're near a sanctuary." He rips my bonds off and plucks me up, then pushes me in front of him and painfully pins my arms behind me. "Let's go."

I'm led off the plane into a private airfield that is absolutely pitch black. There are no lights anywhere. It looks like an abandoned military base.

There's a shack in the distance that he brings me to. The inside is small and cramped. A tiny bed sits in one corner and a broken chair is on the other side.

James shoves me through the door. He tries the lock, but it's rusted. It snaps under his strength.

He shrugs. "I don't think you're dumb enough to run," he tells me. "If you try, you know what will happen. So don't."

He slams the door shut and leaves me in the dark.

Luckily I can see. I go to the window and watch him as he begins to refuel the plane.

He told me before we were making a stop in Russia. Is this it? What's our final destination?

I shiver. I thought escaping The Haven would free me. I had no idea what was waiting for me next.

James returns after an hour. He stands near the door with his arms crossed. I sit still on the bed.

I can feel a vibration in the air. There's some type of resonance between us, almost like a thrumming. I'm unsure what to make of it, or what could be the cause.

"Stop that," he snarls.

I give a stare. "What?"

"You know what. Don't test me." He sounds testy.

"I'm not doing anything!" I protest.

"Like hell you aren't." He takes a menacing step forward. "You're playing your tricks on me, witch, as if you think I don't realize—"

A massive crash sounds in the distance. Both our heads whip to it.

"What was that?" I gasp.

James runs to the window. A low rumble fills the air, but this one is coming from outside.

"That," he growls, "Is your ill-timed rescue party."

He seizes me by the neck and hauls me out the door.

Chapter Forty-Eight

RAUL

Mother proves to be a willing ally... when her interests align with mine.

I run to her as soon as I discover that Eleira's been taken, and James is back. I thought I'd have to convince her to lend me her help, but when she understood what had happened, she quickly consents.

She ignores the issue of holding Phillip hostage as if it didn't exist, however.

She gives me a GPS tracker bewitched to show Eleira's location. I get the distinct impression that casting that spell on it takes nearly all of her remaining strength.

As soon as I have it, I'm off to the nearest airfield to get the fastest jet I can find. James wasn't the only one of the Soren brothers to learn how to fly.

Mother also did me another favor right before I left. She gave me a small, precious stone she picked from the cliffs enchanted with the wards that keep The Haven hidden from the world. She said the stone would extend the ward's protection—namely, invisibility—to anything within a fifty-foot radius of it for as long as the magic lasted inside.

I asked her how long that would be. She couldn't answer exactly, but said it was enough to cloak my jet and follow James without being exposed.

And so I track Eleira's signal from the cockpit of my plane. It comes to a stop on a deserted piece of land in Eastern Russia. I recognize the coordinates as an old airbase, long since abandoned.

It's my chance to catch up.

Yet mere minutes before my arrival the stone's magic gives out. There comes a crash like a sonic boom as my fighter jet bursts through the protective field.

I curse, knowing I've lost the element of surprise—but I'm close enough that James cannot escape.

I land the jet and jump outside. I spot a decrepit building in the distance.

In the doorway, holding Eleira by the neck, stands James.

"So," he sneers. "You've come for her, after all."

I walk toward them, my eyes focused on him. Once I get within a half-dozen meters, he holds up a hand.

"Uh-uh-uh," he utters. He extends his claws and presses them against Eleira's neck. "Come no closer, brother. Or your precious girl dies."

"You wouldn't," I say. Still, I remain in place.

"Do you want to try me?" One finger scratches the faintest mark on Eleira's neck. She gasps and tenses.

"See what I wouldn't do, Raul," he says. "You don't know who I am, what I've seen, or what I'm destined to become."

We start to circle each other.

"I saw father, did you know?" he continues. "I saw him, and I left his coven *alive*. How's that for a feat?"

"Did you kill him?" I demanded. I have to engage him in conversation to buy myself and Eleira more time. The alternative, embracing my darkness, and using *it* as the propelling force for the rescue, is too ghastly to think about. "Did you do what Mother tasked you with?"

He laughs. "No," he says. "I could not. The power Father

wields, Raul, it's unbelievable. You should have seen it. You should have witnessed his glory."

"Let the girl go," I tell him. "You don't need her."

"Oh, but that's where you're wrong." His claws dig deeper into her neck, puncturing her skin almost enough to draw blood. She's pale as a ghost. "Eleira is *precisely* the one I need, and I intend to have her. I'm not going to let you stop me."

"James, we're *brothers*," I say. "Surely you can see why we need to cooperate. We —"

He cuts me off with a roar of laughter. "Diplomacy was never your strong point," he mocks. "You think you can appeal to me with your words?" He scoffs. "Hardly."

But then he holds out his free hand.

"And yet... you can join me, brother. It can be you and I who inherit The Crypts. Forget The Haven. There is nothing there for us. You and I can rise and rule together. Together, we can control the greatest coven in the world!"

We continue circling one another other, like two cats in a scrapyard. Eleira is the unwitting prize.

"You would have me?" I say, not bothering to conceal my incredulity. "I doubt that. You love no one but yourself, James. You would betray your own family to get a step up."

"Oh, but you know me too well," he smiles sadly. "And yet, you still think you can wrest Eleira from me?"

"What do you want with her?" I demand.

"The same thing everyone wants, it seems." The distance between us is getting smaller. "I want her for her gifts."

I catch her eye. For a scant second, I see the utmost fear in them.

And then that fear is pushed down deep and replaced by a steely courage.

I marvel at her ability to remain so strong, to have so much resilience.

"You know who she is to Mother," I say. "You know that our Queen would do anything to get her back."

"Our Queen sends you. You, and you alone. Where is her royal guard? Why do they not accompany you? Why are they not here for her rescue?" He laughs. "No, Raul, what I think is that it's *you* who wants Eleira for himself. You've been addicted to her scent since I brought her to us from her university."

"You risk angering the most powerful vampire in existence," I warn. "Wait until you see Mother's true wrath."

James laughs again. "Mother? You think *Mother* is the most powerful alive?"

"You know she is," I growl. "And she has magic—"

"The same *magic* that keeps her bound in The Haven!" James erupts. "The same magic that keeps her prisoner inside its walls!"

My eyes narrow.

"You did not know?" James seems genuinely surprised. "Why else would she be so desperate for a successor?" He thrusts Fleira forward. "Why else would she treasure this dumb, vapid, useless teen girl so?"

The anger inside me rises at every insult he flings Eleira's way. I have to keep it under control, together with the darkness, or else...

"You think Mother wants to give up her rule, Raul? If so, you are more a fool than I knew. She will keep control of The Haven and use Eleira as a mere surrogate. She will chain her inside the castle and draw on her powers while she lives free. You claim you care for Eleira, and yet you would subject her to such a future? What I offer her..." he brings his mouth closer to her ear and wraps an arm around her body to tug her into him. "What I offer you, my dear," he whispers to her, "is freedom. Freedom from the hell you would find with Raul. Freedom from the slavery Mother would put you through. But ultimately… it's all your choice."

Everything happens at once.

James releases Eleira and pushes her forward. At the same time, an enormous spotlight flares to life and hits me like a laser beam.

Eleira stumbles and falls. Her palms scrape against the ground. The skin tears, and blood, her sweet, precious blood, pours out.

The scent of it befuddles my senses.

But I can't react, because the spotlight has some sort of UV bulbs in it, making it feel just like the sun. As soon as the light hits me, the worst pain I've ever known erupts over my body.

I roar and try to jump out of the way but my knees buckle from the pain. The bright rays make it impossible to open my eyes. My skin starts burning, and I open my mouth to scream in pure agony.

Half a second is all I get, half a second of torture as my skin sizzles and smokes and burns, and then the spotlight switches off.

Exactly at that moment, James collides with me.

He crashes into my midsection and flattens me on the ground. I'm trapped beneath him, but I feel my strength returning. It's a strength fuelled by anger. I use his momentum and flip him off me, then roll to my feet —

And am blindsided when somebody catches me from behind. A sack is shoved over my head, and it somehow cuts off all of my senses, my sight, my hearing, my orientation...

Silver.

Two cuffs close around my wrists. A foot is planted to my back and I go sprawling. I struggle against the sack, trying desperately to spring myself free.

"Raul! Raul, no!" Eleira is screaming for me. Then her screams turn to shrieks that quickly fade as she's carried away.

"Eleira!" I cry. "Elei—"

A heavy, metal object swings into my heard. I topple with the blow.

Then there's silence.

I drift.

For the longest time, I don't know if I'm conscious or not. The sack cuts everything off, even the sensation to my body. The sense of my failure washes over me.

If only I'd embraced the darkness, I think. *If only I hadn't been so reluctant...*

Somebody pulls me up. "Steady," a thick, female voice says. It's muffled by the sack. "Hold him still. There we go..."

A few moments pass, and then the sack is torn off.

I blink, disoriented. I'm still in the middle of the airfield. Eleira is nowhere to be seen.

There is, however, a short, sensual, blonde woman in front of me.

Immediately, I sense her strength. My jaw drops. She's powerful. Viciously so. Stronger than James or me or Mother.

She smiles and kneels down to touch my cheek. "So pretty," she murmurs. She turns my head this way and that. "With hair like fire. And eyes a-blazing."

The natural vampire instincts within me command me to defer, to kneel down, to bow my head. I fight against them with every bit of willpower I possess.

But such strength radiates from her. I've never before been awed by a vampire's presence.

Until now.

Who is this?

She lets go, stands, and looks behind me. "Do it," she says.

I gasp as a sharp needle is jabbed into my neck. All goes black.

Chapter Forty-Nine

RAUL

I wake up in a dark, cold prison cell.

My hands are stretched above me. My wrists are bound by silver chains. They burn into my flesh.

I thrash to break free. The chains whip against the wall but don't give. I summon all my strength, and pull, and *pull...*

The mortar the chain is attached to gives. I jerk forward. I grit my teeth, straining, and try again.

I give a massive yank and the chain rips free from the wall. Bits of stone rain down on me. The block the chain was attached to smashes into the ground with a monstrous crash. The room shakes from the impact.

I'm breathing hard, but at least now I have control of my hands. They are bound in front of me and a never-ending darkness lies beyond. Even with my sight I cannot see all the way to the end.

I approach the bars of my prison. I look at them from up close but do not dare to touch. They are also silver. Meant for keeping a vampire inside.

I do a quick scan of the room, searching the walls for a weakness. I find nothing. I'm not surprised, but I *am* curious where I am.

Are these the holding cells of The Crypts?

What else could they be? Unless I'm in some other coven—a coven that petite blonde vampire belongs to.

Alarm seizes me. *Eleira!* Where is she?

I yell her name. My voice echoes in darkness and then fades.

Nobody answers my call.

I wait a long time. I'd managed to break the chains from the wall. But what else can I apply my strength to? I can't dig my way out, cannot break through those impenetrable silver bars...

Distant footsteps catch my attention. Slowly, they get closer and closer.

I stare out into the black, expecting to find my brother. Instead, I see the blonde.

She grins and cocks her head to one side. "Sticks and stones may break your bones, but rock will never hurt you." She laughs. "Good thing silver is a universal weakness."

"Who are you? What do you want?" I take an angry step forward, fighting against the sphere of influence her strength exerts over me. "Where is Eleira?"

"The girl is safe enough. Don't you fret. It's *you* we're concerned about."

I say nothing.

She sighs. "Your Father would be pleased to see you. In fact, I think he'd be fascinated that I managed to bring two of his sons to him. Too bad he doesn't know a thing about your arrival."

So I am in The Crypts.

"It's too bad I didn't meet you first. You *are* the more handsome of the pair."

"How long are you going to keep me here?"

"Straight to the point, huh?" She flips her hair back. "You aren't the tiniest bit taken in by me? A little bit of flirtation is always fun…" she trails off. "But I forget. You only have eyes for the girl. I heard how loud you screamed for her. Oh, how touching it was. Really, it broke my heart." She puts her hands over her chest.

"Let's just hope she feels the same way about you."

The woman steps to the side and punches in a code on the lock pad. Immediately the silver bars slide up.

I'm free.

Do I dare make a break for it? I look into the darkness again. I can try, but I'm sure she'll catch me. I have a definitive impression of her strength, her speed, an intuitive awareness of all her powers.

If I run, she would catch me, and it would only anger her.

So instead, I take a step to her. "What now?"

She smirks and picks up the chain holding my wrists. She doesn't even flinch as the silver touches her skin. "I'm going to bring you to Eleira now," she says. "And we'll see the extent of your devotion."

Chapter Fifty

ELEIRA

I come to in a dank and frigid place deep beneath the earth.

Immediately, I sense a presence nearby. I open my eyes and see James.

He's leering at me from across the room.

"Finally," he says. "I was beginning to wonder how long it would take you to rise." He strolls toward me. I shy back, then remember my resolve and steady myself.

He touches my cheek, then traces the back of his fingers down my neck. "Sleeping beauty," he murmurs.

I want to recoil, but I won't give him the pleasure of seeing how he affects me.

Suddenly, all the memories of the fight come back. "Raul!" I gasp. "What did you do to him? What—"'

"My brother is in good hands," James says. There's a note of... bitterness... in his voice? "I must say I find it disheartening you inquire about him and not me."

"You're a monster," I spit.

"Oh, and you will be one too, quite soon, my dear."

I try to move my arms but they're bound behind me tight.

"What is this place?"

"You're in my room," he says. "In my Father's coven." James brings his face close to mine and takes a deep breath. "He would be *so pleased* that I brought him a witch."

I try to snap at him but he smoothly steps back. "What do you want from me?"

"Nothing that you're incapable of giving." James smiles. "Ah, I think I hear our guests."

Sure enough, a few moments later, the door opens. The woman vampire from the airfield comes in. She has a silver chain wrapped in her arms. She gives it a tug, and Raul stumbles in, growling at her in anger.

Then he sees me. "Eleira!" he exclaims. My heart blooms with joy at seeing him safe and unharmed. And the strangest sensation of nerves settles into my stomach. I've never felt its like before.

"What a happy reunion this is," the woman vampire says. She closes the door, and all four of us are locked in. "Forgive me. I should introduce myself. I'm Victoria—"

"How could you?" Raul is staring daggers at his brother. "How could you betray us?"

Victoria gives him a nasty look for cutting her off. But James speaks.

"Betray you? No, no. I saw a better way. For too long you and I and Phillip have been tied to Mother's apron strings. *This* grants us freedom. *This* will give us true power."

Raul scoffs. "You're blinded by ambition. Mother is keeping Phillip hostage. She'll *kill him* if Eleira doesn't return by the next full moon."

My heart sinks. Is *that* the reason he came for me? To save his brother? To bring me back, and enter me in... The Hunt?

James, give him credit, is taken aback. "She wouldn't—"

"Oh yes," Raul says. "She would."

"Enough of this," Victoria hisses in annoyance. "We're here to do one thing. Let's get on with it."

James seems energized by her command. He grabs my neck,

and I cry out. Raul dashes toward me to help. He doesn't get more than half a step before Victoria yanks him back by the chain.

"None of that," she says. "We need the two of you apart."

She pulls him to the far opposite wall, where two pegs are embedded in the rock. She hooks the chain on, even as Raul struggles against it. She makes it look so easy, manhandling a grown vampire like that. Not to mention that Raul is so much bigger than her.

Could she be a witch? I wonder. *Is that why he cannot fight back?*

After a moment of snarled curses and grunts Raul's arms are spread to either side of him like he's being crucified. Victoria pulls on the chains, and Raul's feet leave the ground. He's hanging only from those pegs.

My own struggle against the hand hanging around my neck seems feeble and pathetic in comparison. James holds me as easily as if I were a child.

Raul starts to rage against Victoria.

She slaps him.

"You be quiet," she snaps. "Or next time, I'll take it out on your beloved." She looks at me.

Beloved? I wonder.

"Now," Victoria pulls a table up between us. Onto it she sets a series of four medieval goblets. "Four chalices," she explains. "And four of us. What a striking coincidence."

James has a knowing smirk on his face. Raul is scowling but quiet. I'm just confused.

"We all know blood is key to our power," Victoria continues. "And that blood, when imbued with the proper elements, can transfer that power."

James's eyes take on a greedy sheen. He grips my neck tighter.

Victoria looks at me. "We need you to be strong for what is to come. Your current human form… it just won't do. I can see from your eyes the transformation has begun. But we need to expedite the process."

"No!" Raul gasps.

"Silence!" Victoria barks. "Another word out of you, and I'm not kidding, I *will* hurt her. Or don't you think," she asks sweetly, "that I can sense the allure of her blood too?"

Victoria nods at James. "Bring her forward."

I cry out as James pushes me to the table. He grabs my wrist and thrusts it out. Victoria withdraws a small, silver dagger.

Before I know it, she slashes my wrist.

I scream. Blood pours out. James forces it over the first of the chalices. It fills the cup. Raul struggles like crazy against his bonds, trying to break free. But the silver is impossibly strong.

Yet the scent of my blood enrages him. He yells and screams and throws his body forward. He fights the chains like a demon trying to break out of hell.

James, at the same time, goes absolutely still. His gaze latches onto the blood pouring from my wrist as he moves it from one chalice to the next. I can tell it takes his all to hold back.

The precariousness of my situation hits me with full force. I'm alone in a room with three vampires. Human blood is their weakness. Mine has, for whatever reason, extraordinary appeal.

And I'm bleeding freely before them.

The only one who seems unaffected is Victoria. And yet... and yet the way she licks her lips, while watching me bleed, it's...

Terrifying.

My heart is beating so hard in my chest that the sound is all I hear. There's a long, tense moment as the last of the cups is filled. Victoria's eyes are on me.

And then she says, "Enough!"

As if a spell is cast James is flung backward. I'm free, but only for a moment. Victoria speeds forward and clamps a gauntlet over my wrist. It stems the blood flow.

All three vampires visibly relax. Raul goes still, but keeps panting. He directs a haunted glare at Victoria. He purposefully avoids my eyes.

James returns and brings me back to the far wall.

"My turn," Victoria says. She uses that dagger to prick a finger. Into each goblet goes one drop of her blood.

She motions James over. "Now yours…"

Each time a drop of vampiric blood mixes with mine in a chalice, a loud, violent hissing sounds. There's a ritualistic, dark quality to the way the ceremony is being performed. It makes me ill at ease.

"Finally," Victoria turns to Raul. "It's your turn."

"No!" he says. "No, I will not let you! No—"

"Oh, brother," James interrupts. "You speak as if you have a choice."

The dagger flashes. Raul's forearm is cut. Victoria brings the goblets one-by-one to him, and holds them by his elbow to catch the flow. His blood joins ours in the bowls.

"And now we wait," she says.

Raul continues to bleed. I don't know why he's not healing. But as more and more blood flows out of him, he starts to sag and weaken.

He turns his head to James. His eyes are rolling in his head. "Please," he implores. "Don't let her do this."

James looks at him. I think I see the briefest flash of pity in his eyes.

Then he laughs. "You think I don't want this as much as her?"

"Want what?" I scream. I'm as helpless to change anything as a newborn lamb, but that doesn't mean I don't want answers.

James clamps a hand over my mouth. "Shut it," he warns.

"I know you have good in you," Raul implores. "Deep down. I know you do. Don't forsake us all!"

"Forsake you?" James sounds livid. "I asked you to join me,

brother! I have not forsaken anyone. It is you who's turned his back on me! And for what?" He glares at me. "For some snivelling teenage girl? Please."

"Enough!" Victoria claps her hands. "It is done. The fusion is complete." She looks at me, and her eyes positively shine with lust. "Now, the real fun begins."

Chapter Fifty-One

ELEIRA

A rag is stuffed into my mouth so I cannot scream. Some sort of velvet bag is thrust over Raul's head, and as soon as it happens his movements become uncoordinated, jerky, almost convulsive. I want to yell for him, but before I get the chance the same sort of bag is thrown over my head.

Immediately, the strangest sensation takes me. It's like I'm caught between two reverberating speakers operating at different frequencies. It's jarring, and I want to fight it, but I'm helpless to do anything.

James grabs me by the arm and marches me out the room. I can only vaguely tell where we're going. The sense of direction I usually have is somehow... blurred. It's hazy.

We walk for I don't know how long. Even sounds are muffled. I don't think we come across anybody else.

Eventually, we stop. The cover over my head is cast off. And I find us in...

An enormous treasure vault.

My eyes pop out my head. There are piles upon piles of gleaming gold coins around us. They're stacked shoulder-high by the walls. In their midst I see rubies and diamonds and all types of precious stones.

The riches spill out onto the floor. There isn't a square inch that isn't covered with wealth.

There's a fire burning on the other side of one of the great piles. It makes shadows flicker and dance over everything. It gives the vault a menacing air, almost like we're inside a dragon's den.

Victoria clears a space in front of us. Raul sits slumped on the ground, the sack still over his head.

His limbs twitch. Once, twice, three times. Then he goes still for a moment, and then starts convulsing again.

I can't take it. He's obviously in pain. "What are you doing to him?" I try to say. The rag muffles all words.

James shares a look with Victoria. She nods. He takes the nasty cloth out of my mouth.

"But," he says precisely, putting a finger against my lips be-

fore I can speak. "If you so much as think of screaming, you —
and my brother — will both be punished. Understand?"

I move my head up and down, burning with hatred for the
vampire, him and his evil companion.

When I was first caught, I thought all vampires were evil. But
now, as I stand on the verge of becoming one of them, I'm starting
to figure out that is not the case.

Evil is not absolute. It's not black and white.

Raul and Phillip, for example, are far less evil than their older brother. Or Victoria.

"What's wrong with him?" I demand when James pulls his
finger back.

He shrugs casually. "Silver meshing, in the fabric." He motions above his head to mimic the sack. "Silver screws with a
vampire's mind and senses."

I look down at the one that was over my head.

"Ah yes, little one," he acknowledges. "You are vulnerable,
too. The effects are not as strong... yet." He glances at Victoria,
who's laid out the four chalices in a circle on the floor. Right in
the middle is an enormous red ruby. "But they will be soon."

"What do you mean?" I gasp.

"We're going to expedite your transformation," Victoria says. She smiles. "And then you'll be putty in our hands."

Something triggers Raul into a series of very strong spasms. I hear him grunt and groan, and his body shakes.

"Get it off him!" I plead. "Please, take it off! If you do, I won't fight. If you do —" I hang my head. "I'll give you what you want."

James's eyebrows go up. "An interesting proposition," he says. "Victoria?"

She shrugs. "If she reneges, it'll be easy to make her regret it."

James smiles. "Very well."

He walks up to my brother and goes to his knees by his side. He puts a hand on Raul's shoulder.

Then he brings his lips close to Raul's covered ear.

"Your human," he says softly, "is worried about you. Isn't that sweet?" He tugs the cloth sack off.

Immediately, Raul gasps for air. His hair is dishevelled, his eyes wild, as he struggles against his chains.

Then he sees where he is. He sees the riches around him. And he sees me.

He goes still.

"Do whatever you want to me," he tells James. "But let Eleira go."

James laughs. "Funny. She just offered a similar concession for you."

Raul looks at me. Our eyes meet. I feel something very heart-felt in his gaze.

"We're not going to let her go," Victoria says. "But we *will* make her one of us. And when she is..." she smiles cruelly. "She will be no more than a pawn, ready to do anything I say."

"*We* say," James corrects.

Victoria touches his cheek. "No, dearest," she tells him. "*I* say. The rule of power still stands."

I can feel James's agitation at being addressed so. But he keeps his lips sealed.

Victoria turns to me. "You said you'd do anything, didn't you? Then step forward. You must be the first to drink our blood."

Victoria yanks me by the shirt. I stumble but do not fall.

She shoves me to my knees before the arrangement of chalices. Raul's protests continue in the background. "No! Don't do this, no, no..."

"Shut him up," Victoria snarls.

James thrusts the bag back over his head.

I cry out. "You promised! You —"

"You, too, girl." Victoria grabs my hair. "If you value your own life, you will drink."

She shoves a chalice into my hands. "Now, do it!"

I look at the revolting fluid sloshing around inside. Raul's screams sound through the sack. "Eleira, no! Eleira, don't!"

"You have no choice!" Victoria hisses. "Do it now, before I force you to it!"

I'm shaking all over. I don't know what will happen to me once I drink. Raul seems to know, and he thinks it's bad.

I take a breath and catch a whiff of the blood. It smells horrid. *Why do they want me to drink first?* I wonder. *Why —*

"Oh, for crying out loud," Victoria exclaims and shoves the goblet to my lips.

As soon as the blood passes my tongue… a force takes me. My eyes go wide. A roaring desire explodes inside to have more. I clutch at the chalice and take deep, gulping swallows. The blood goes down my throat and burns like acid. But even as it burns, it energizes me, making me feel a new vigor, a new strength coming over my body.

The cup is empty too soon. I'm ravenous. My eyes dart to the other three. Something is happening inside my body, some sort of *shift*. I feel the cells changing. I feel my senses becoming stronger, more alive. I feel my muscles strengthening. It's the kind of solid, all-encompassing strength that comes with an innate knowledge of my capabilities.

I lunge for the second goblet. "Hold her back!" James screams. "That's ours!"

Victoria tries to catch me, but I throw her off. I'm operating on instinct alone, and instinct tells me that all of this is mine— that all of these vampires are *mine*.

I grab the next chalice and quickly empty it. Victoria tries to come at me again. I'm in a rage, and I toss her sideways as easily as if she were a doll.

There's power inside me. Deep, latent power. Power I didn't

know existed before, but power that has now been unleashed.

In my brief pause, as I grapple with my staggering strength, James and Victoria both throw themselves at me. Their claws are out, and they're snarling and trying to hold me down. I fight against them. I'm strong, but I'm still only one, and they are two...

A blinding flash explodes from the ruby. The light is like a solid wall. It hits and throws all three of us back. We crash into the piles of coins, and they go flying.

"You idiot!" Victoria screams at me. "What did you do, what did you —"

It's mayhem all around. The blast hit Raul and knocked the sack off his head. He comes to and sees what's happening. His silver bonds have broken.

Did the light do that, too?

"SHE'S TOO STRONG!" James is yelling somewhere in the distance. "VICTORIA, YOU CAN'T —"

The words are lost on me as I'm consumed by the undeniable urge to feed. My body demands it. There's blood available in the chalices—somehow, they were unaffected by the blast—but a different scent calls to me.

The scent of evil.

I turn to Victoria.

It comes from her.

There's genuine fear in her eyes. She backs away. "No, no, don't..."

Before I know what's happening I launch myself at her. I no longer have conscious control over my body. Everything happens by instinct, by feel. I have her in my arms, and my lips curl back, revealing two long, glistening fangs —

"Eleira!"

Raul's voice snaps me to myself. I stop. For a half second, I oscillate between awareness of what I'm doing and that complete blackout.

But then the animal inside me roars, and I'm about to sink my fangs into Victoria's smooth, perfect neck —

"No."

Raul again. His voice carries true command. Once more I stop. I waver between who I was and who I've become. I can feel my humanity hanging by a string. If I lose control now...

"...If you lose control now," Raul is saying. I realize those aren't my thoughts but his words. They mix and swirl in my head. "If you kill Victoria now, there is no going back. Eleira, no. Eleira, don't do it."

I look at the feeble woman struggling in my arms. She seems so weak, so very fragile. I could snap her like a twig.

And yet, just moments ago I was in awe of her power.

James is watching all of this with fascination clear on his face. Fascination and stark disbelief.

Raul takes a step toward me. Victoria has gone still. Fear lurks in her eyes.

"Don't do this," Raul says softly. "It is not the only way."

He puts a hand on my arm. I expect him to be cold.

Instead, I feel warmth flow from him.

"You're confused by the bloodlust," he tells me. "This isn't you. This isn't who you would be."

"How do you know?" I snarl, and I barely recognize my own voice. It comes from deep inside, from that animalistic, vampiric part the drink of blood unleased.

"I know," Raul says softly, "because I've seen your heart. I know who you are. And once, in a different life, I gave you... this."

From his back pocket he takes out a black onyx ring. It's enormous, nearly the size of a quail egg.

My breath catches. I recognize it. It's something I had as a child. I'd always loved it, always adored it. I'd treasured it, and worn it round my neck always... until I lost it when I turned thirteen.

"It was supposed to shield you," Raul explains. He shoots a look at James. "It was supposed to protect you from us. I saw the signs of your birth, and I sought you out before Mother knew. I wanted to save you from this life. Had you worn it, none of us could have found you. None of this," he gestures around, "would have happened."

"Traitor!" James snarls. "*You* went against us —"

I shut him up with a single look. I can feel his strength, and it's so much less than mine.

My eyes soften for Raul. "You... tried to protect me?"

"Yes," he admits. "Always, I wanted to be your guardian. Why did you stop wearing it, Eleira? Why did you take it off?"

"I... I thought I lost it."

"And now it's found." He takes a cautious step toward me.

"Let Victoria go." He holds out his hand. "Let her go, and come with me. I'll get you out of here. You will be safe."

I hesitate. I *have* to feed…. but it's an instinctual desire. Rationally, *feeding* repulses me.

"Fools," Victoria laughs. She glares at me and Raul, defiant now. "You think she can ever be safe? She's a *witch,* and now amongst the most powerful vampires alive." She turns her head up to me. "Do it! Feed on me, kill me, take my blood!"

"No," Raul says. "Come to me, Eleira. Take your ring. It can't protect you from us anymore, but it will help."

I'm torn. Never before have I so desired two polar opposite things.

Victoria's taunts continue unabated.

Raul's hand is held out for me.

I look at the vampire in my grasp. I can end her, I know I can. I have the power, I have the strength —

"*Please,*" Raul says. "Don't lose yourself. Please."

With a staggered lurch, I let go of Victoria and grab Raul's hand. He pulls me into him. He holds me tight. Such warmth flows from his body… and I know, I just know, that it's fuelled by love.

He strokes my hair. I fall into him. In his arms, I feel safe. I feel protected. The vampiric instincts are still raging inside me, but I can temper them down.

He takes my hand and slips the ring on. Right away it all becomes easier. The lust for blood, the craving to feed, to feast, to *kill*... it all eases.

The scent of evil fades. Had I mistaken it before? Was I projecting it *onto* Victoria, whereas in reality, it did not exist?

I look into Raul's eyes. He's staring at me as if he's found a long-lost lover.

"You are the same," he whispers. "And I've been waiting so long for you."

And then he moves his head down, and his lips touch mine. And all my inhibition fade, all my uncertainties vanish, as I share in that life-giving kiss.

Chapter Fifty-Two

I let Eleira go. She stares up at me, looking so sweet and endearing, with her lips red and puffy from our kiss, that I can't imagine how I've managed to resist her for this long.

She is the one. I fought it before, fought the knowledge buried deep inside me. But she is my love, reincarnated in this life just as the celestial charts predicted.

I'd saved Liana from her fate. She would have been my Mother's pawn if Morgan knew the truth of her birth. I tried to do the same with Eleira...

But some things are not meant to be. Or rather, maybe *this* is how it's meant to be, and I'm supposed to share in this life with the woman I love.

I don't know. Yet I'm sure Eleira has feelings for me, maybe not to the extent of mine for her, but that's because she doesn't *know* yet.

We have a lifetime to uncover them.

"What happens now?" she asks me softly. She glances back at James and Victoria.

"They defer to you," I say. "The vampire hierarchy makes it so. They won't do anything that you prohibit."

Her eyes widen in wonder.

"But I suggest," I say, "that we escape this place and go back to The Haven. What I said about Phillip —"

"Yes," she nods. I can see the gears turning in her head. "Yes, I don't want anything to happen to him. Then there's April, and the others…"

James perks up at the mention of his human lover. Victoria casts him a nasty frown.

"You're in no threat from The Hunt," I say. "Not as a vampire. But there are other threats lurking. I won't be able to protect you from them all."

"I don't need your protection," she says harshly. But then her eyes soften. "Yet… I wouldn't mind your guidance."

"I'll give it," I promise.

Then I bring her into my arms and kiss her once more.

The End

THANK YOU FOR READING!

Want More of The Vampire Gift?

The Vampire Gift 2 comes out June 2016!

Don't want to miss it? Sign up for my mailing list (http://eepurl.com/bYCp41) to get an email the day it comes out!

Loved the book? Let me know by leaving a review on Amazon! Or come say hi to me on Facebook – I love meeting and interacting with my fans :)

www.Facebook.com/AuthorEMKnight

Free Book Offer!

Want to get the next book in The Vampire Gift series for free? Here's how you do it...

1. Leave a review on Amazon.com for *The Vampire Gift 1: Wards of Night.*

2. Once the review is posted, email me a link to it with the subject "Free Book Offer". My email: em@emknight.com

3. As soon as the next book comes out, I'll send you a special link to download the book for free! You can request any book in the series as your free "thank you" book.

Made in the USA
Middletown, DE
31 October 2016